LorD oF CHAOS

ISBN: 978-1-7397708-8-4

First edition.

First published in 2023 by Erratum Press
Sheffield, UK
www.erratumpress.com

Interior design by Mike Corrao
Cover and cover image by Ansgar Allen

Excerpts of *Lord of Chaos* first appeared in various incantations in the following publications: "Old Lady Talking to Time" in *Surfaces.cx;* "Zone 1: Imagined Poverty & Likenesses / Apple Sauce & Cancerous Breasts" at *Misery Tourism;* "Limbs Amidst Time / The Poet & the Great Philosopher King" in *Youngmag;* "Zone 4: Clinical Lycanthropy / La Bocca al Lupo" at *Expat Press;* "There Was a Place in My Neck Where Meaning Once Stood" in *HARSHLitMag.*

LORD OF CHAOS

Daniel Beauregard

ERRATUM PRESS

Eye ravening patient in the haggard vulture face,
perhaps it's carrion time

                    - Samuel Beckett, Texts for Nothing

PART ONE — THE VOID

I was aloof in the void for what seemed like nothing because
I knew nothing but nothing. There was the void, which was
nothing; nothing but the void; which is something; until
suddenly I perceived something apart from the void, perhaps,
another presence in the void that hadn' t been there prior.
This other something helped me to better understand the void
as if to better understand myself in understanding something
outside of nothing, or aside from nothing; something other
than the void, that is, aside from the void itself, which
solidified that not everything was part of the void, that in
the void there could be something, even though the void itself
was nothing but immense.

I like the idea that something vacuous and indescribable
can nevertheless exist; it comforted me while I was feeling
the emptiness of the void, how inside the void there was
another something other than it, the void, in which I felt
comfort, which became something in itself. Because of that
something known as comfort I was confronted with an excuse to
think outside of the void; how apart from its all-consuming
emptiness, there were ideas apart from the void, a fact which
changed my perception of the void itself; although in the
moment I knew I actually knew nothing but what the void might
be and a vague idea of something lingering apart.

It was the Time in the void alone that accompanied me.
Although there was no way of directly feeling Time, as it was
apart from the void nonetheless; not nothing but something
unvoidlike itself, in the sense that its lingering presence
persisted when I lingered on the presence of Time not lost
in the void but there within me, as a concept. Perhaps the
void had planned for this. Perhaps the void planned for Time
to float above, there along with me, in the void; a linear

expansion to its condition. I' m now aware that I' ve been
in the void for millions of moments such as this, all of them
lost in the void without meaning but nevertheless persistent
and present, which makes me think perhaps the void wasn' t
a void at all, or isn' t now; perhaps it urges me to pursue
these unvoidlike things inside myself, while imagining them
existing as well outside me. This presence of time in the
void, for instance, I imagined, as perhaps something only
there within myself, as if I' m capable of producing such
powerful items. As if I' m capable of producing such things
within—and in my relation to—the void as it remains, a state
wherein perhaps the more powerful things I produce, I might
as well believe, the less immense the void becomes. I then
felt the void expanding, opening, in spite of such thinking;
or I became aware of something moving alongside me, aware of
movement, however unvoidlike that may seem. It may have been
my own will to move that I had felt, I can' t quite recall,
but either way, I was thereby thrown headlong into Pain;
hurling through something that was hurting, something either
outside of the void or inside the void, but not of the void,
or so I felt; it was my own Feeling, I imagined, another
something.

How unvoidlike, so I scoffed, thereby frightening my own
existence; wherein attempting to locate the location of this
Pain I became aware that I was even more than something,
that from the void I was quite apart; that wherein as I could
control my movement inside the void, I was also able to mimic
the idea of the expanding void by reaching out and touching
the condition of my Pain before me, as in with an extension
of my person, which we might call a limb. This action was
a revelation and further distinguished an area among the
void that seemed like something all my own, as though inside
the void I could now think of myself as a piece apart from

it, in which if the void was removed, I might become my own
protrusion, both from myself and my relation to the void,
which made me force myself to think about whether my relation
to the void had something to do with the void itself.

I began to test this concept, pushing through the void with my
limbs, proceeding forward, backward, or sideways in relation
to the void I was aware of beneath my feet, as well the void
around my body, which supported both my body and my mind. I
felt my way forward, pushing through the void in Time, as only
Time allowed; where time can only move forward, into the void;
where Time pushes in its relation to the very void itself,
forcing it to expand around it, to become more than a void, or
more so a void, a void greater through its ability to spread.
This unvoidlike process had begun—Time—whether through my
unvoidlike procession through the void or simply in being
thought of, or felt, through Pain, inside myself or things
unto their own, as voids apart from what the void was. I find
it troubles me to think; it troubles me to question, in my
relation to the void, these things, which may only be empty,
devoid of meaning, until an awareness ascribes it to them for
purposes unknown. Has the void planned for this as well? I
have no answer.

I move my limbs to touch my Pain. I feel my Pain rise and
wriggle through my body, whereas each Time I push forward,
my own void screams in relation both to the void beneath my
feet and the void inside my mind. I proceed nonetheless,
even now, bearing the unbearable Pain in ongoing unvoidlike fashion until after a Time the Pain subdues, or grows
dulled by the immensity of the full brunt of the nothing
as I continue there within it, determined to explore its
unopen spaces as we proceed.

Can the void hear? If it can, should I be wary? For it has
eaten my ideas once before, I think. There was a Time, one
unlike this voidlike Time, another void where Time passed
like a Time unlike a void unto itself; a marked Time, full
of the passage of things, ripened by ideas. That marked
Time is somewhere floating inside me, or I, or along with
me: a Memory not of the void. Perhaps though it is also
nothing, for it exists in the void, which like me, is hindered by emptiness.

It is Cold in the void, I surmise, pushing my way forward
into nothing. I am aware of Cold in the same unvoidlike way
I'm aware of Pain, which is now reduced to nothing more
than a throblike Memory in relation to the immensity of the
void.

The void was as it was for I know not how long, but now
we' re together again: Pain, Time, Thought, the void, I,
fear upon its perch. I' m up against the void that supports
my body, or my body has pressed up against it, more like
was pulled toward it; my limbs feel strange, my little
limbs attached to bigger limbs inside the void turned
stiff. Little clawlike limblets. Miniature versions of
items that gather. Pain, less blinding now, dully reasserts
itself as I begin to move, placing limb and limblet onto
the void in front of me. I push myself up again into
the void but slip on the item protruding from the void
located on myself, and am pulled downward toward the void
supporting my body once again. This time the Pain is
blinding, but the void remains the same.

It has occurred to me that before Thought, Pain, Time—
these things perched above me in the void, swooping down
to frighten my existence—there was only I, therefore, I
posit that these things are voidlike in material, because
only I can give them substance. Only I can feel Pain, mark
the Time. Only the I progresses through the void. Only the
I feels the wetness upon our limblets and thrashes at the
blinding brilliance of our throbbing Pain in its immensity.

Again I kick and find a voidling quite altogether different
from the rest. I kick I kick, and each Time I kick, the
voidling excretes a noise into the void that sounds like
a huuuuuughh. I kick and huuuuuugh. I stop kicking and
press down with my limb directly on top of the voidling and
huuuuughh. I stop pressing for a moment, and the voidling
excretes: huuuuggghhhelp me. I find this excretion strange,
this noise, and press again with my limb; the noise it
excretes this time is much more pronounced. Huuuggghhhelpp

me, I'm in Pain. I pause, releasing the pressure of my
limb from atop the voidling. Pain? It excreted a noise
matching one of my ideas. I am in Pain, I think. I twitch
my limblets where they hold my items to keep from spilling
out into the void anew. I press my limb forcefully down
upon the voidling, which is between my limb and the cold
void that supports my body; I listen to its noises when
I hear them: Pain, again, and hughhhwhhyyyyy. It then
disintegrates with a pop, slicking my limbs with wetness
like the items we hold with our limblets and the other
unmoving voidlings. I make note of it, then I kick. I kick
it out into nothing, to be devoured by the void.

The void is nothing but it is not everything; it is nothing but it is not everything. That's something.

Something is the void beneath my limbs, which feels foreign at some times, familiar at others, as if the void itself was nudging me; at times painful, the void that supports my body now is again Cold, which has settled alongside my Pain. My limbs crunch forward in their relation to the void that supports my body, noising themselves ahead into nothing; noising themselves despite themselves in relation to the resistance of the void's hesitance toward something we know only when we hear it.

My limbs and limblets scrape forward, nudged occasionally by the void that supports my body. The Pain and Time and Thought scatter somewhere up above, swooping to nest nearby and mark the times when our limbs are nudged; scraping inchwards, noising into nothing. What are these contours beneath our limbs? They seem varied, and I mark them as such. And now I pause as Pain swoops down anew, like a dark bird, nudging us to take notice of one of our limbs, which has been lodged in something, or nothing rather, in our relation to the void or my own personal void. Pain travels into our limbs until we clench our limblets, rubbing against the void that supports our body. There is something my limb is lodged in.

Pain skips up and down us as I try to dislodge my limb in its relation to the void; it is difficult and takes much time, for in tandem we hold our items to keep from spilling out of ourselves into nothing. Both the Time and Pain are marked. Something unyielding has lodged my limb in its

relation to the void that supports my body. I scoff into
the void at Time, Pain, Thought, as they perch in nothing.
I refuse to fill them any longer. I refuse to fill these
thoughts—ascribe meaning to them—any longer.

I will not acknowledge Pain, nor the lodging of my limb in
its relation to the void; I will press myself up against
the void that supports my body and go back to the way it
was before, back to the void once passed, the void before
something because it seems these unvoidlike somethings are
only hindrances in my progression through the void. Back
to the void once passed, where items like this weren' t
hindrances: they informed our ideas. Deep inside, we feel
what we know to be a place where Memory has encapsulated
the things that came before. Inarticulate but everpresent.
A collection of things that once held meaning. A gathering
of once-important items deeply buried. If only, we think
now, it could be cracked open, penetrated like the
crumbling voidlings, to explore its empty spaces in search
of meaning. But these hindrances, the ones that persist
before us now, it seems likely that they themselves may be
of the void after all: hollows sent to hinder my progress,
my own expanse. I scream and clench my limblets one last
time, nudge at dislodging my limb from something it hasn' t
been engulfed by in its relation to the void. Nothing. The
void is ever unrelenting.

Lodged into place, all Thought leaves except for Pain.

I try to return to the void once passed. It is everything
and nothing. I am everything and nothing. I feel the void
that supports my body nudging into vacuous areas betwixt
limbs and limblets. It is Cold. Cold inserts itself, lodges
into, like against my limb in its relation to the void.
These hindering lodglings confuse my Thoughts, which I try
now to send into nothing but reassert themselves anew.

Time is marked by Thought, which persists in my relation
to the void despite my attempts at hindering it. The
void has sent these unvoidlike accompaniments, I know. I
know nothing, nothing but the void. I scream, an effort
to send these unvoidlike items back into the void once
passed, again into nothing. Nothing. Time marks nothing,
therefore it is something. At least Thought can be filled
with something. I am nothing, but I can fill Thought with
something. Perhaps in the void before the void, Thought was
thought of as nothing like a hindrance, but something like
Time; this Thought too has passed, after all, out into the
voidlike nothing.

My expansion into the void has ceased, lodged as my limb
is in its relation to the void that supports my body. I am
pressed up against that void, which lodges into the cracks
between my limblets, my little voids, with Cold and Pain in
some places, others absent like the void. Or rather, the
void is the absence of everything, therefore the void is
nothing and I know nothing but the void.

I raise myself up into the void that supports my mind with
my limbs and limblets, forcing them up against the void
that supports my body until I am again alongside Time, Pain
and Thought, perhaps Cold now as well, perched above in the
void that is nothing now like the void once passed; this
I know now, that the void is nothing like the void once
passed. That' s something.

I am something.

Screaming in Pain I progress nothing. In Time I try again. Nothing. Clutching with my limb and limblets to keep the items from falling into the void anew, the warm and sticky items housed inside of us, my limblets became slick with something and Pain makes me howl into the void, we know when we hear it. A crack. Something called a Crack and our limb and limblet is lodged no longer and spills out into the emptiness of the void anew. Little hindrances to mark in our procession, though the voidlings have ceased to present themselves beneath my limbs for I think quite some time. Eaten by the void I surmise. We continue our expansion into the void, often becoming aware of other nudglings beneath our limbs poking into Pain from the void that supports our body.

But almost as soon as we' re released by the Crack, spilling out into the void, progressing once again, another item attracts our attention, a noise that utters nearby. It begins closing in and we halt our expansion to determine its intent. It is a noise like the voidling uttered in the void once passed. It is receding, slipping farther away from us into the nothing. Forgetting all else, we follow it, trailing our balloons behind us. It is leading us to we know not where.

We stumble out into nothing, scraping our limbs on the Cold ground and scratching our items as we fall, lift ourselves up and fall again, as the noise escapes us. But we are determined to mine its empty spaces for answers. For we had that chance in the void once passed, but were unable to exploit it. If we have decided we ourselves exist, then perhaps others like us are in existence as well, pounding the Cold void underfoot in search of answers.

What is passed is now nothing, or no, not quite nothing:
something. The void once passed is as much something then
as it is nothing now, perhaps. Released by a Crack back out
into the void. Our limbs and limblets little lodglings no
longer. The noise upon the wind was nothing.

Little lodglings no longer. Like Thought, Pain, I, Cold
as well now, for we know it when it presses against our
limbs; we scrape it up in our limblets. Cold like nothing.
Familiar like the voidlings, things held over from the void
that once was perhaps. Perhaps not. Perhaps like I thought,
simply somethings to hinder my progression, to keep me
from something. If so, something there is that exists to
be kept from. If so, there is something other than the
void itself, perhaps this is the reason, some reason,
for the hindrances. But is it safe to ask, to make such
assumptions?

Cold scrapes beneath our limbs, leading us along into
nothing, edging, expanding, like these ideas, these things
up there, lodged into space above the void that supports
our body; these hindrances which are somehow something in
their relation to the void, somehow something because they
are not nothing but a hindrance.

Our limbs make a misstep in my relation and we falter, for
a moment things become unstable, as if again all the ideas
came tumbling down on top of our head. In a swoop like Time
one of our limbs finds itself in between the void that
supports our body with the void that supports our mind, its
limblets expanding to hinder Pain from falling down upon
our head. Our limbs find the void that supports our body

but without the presence of Thought, and so our items—what we've been holding inside of us—come spilling out into the void. Pain is everywhere, as if from above it fell and for a moment became the void. Oozing wetness. Nothing but Pain became the void.

And Pain became the void and our items were all upon the void that supports my body, all over again. It is like something so unlike anything from the void once passed, it is everything, as if an item is punching itself through the endless nothing. For a moment it feels like Pain is all there is; in the absence of Thought, Pain is the void once passed, or so it seems.

A Feeling is something that is already filled with Thought,
I think, gathering up the items into our own personal void
once again and holding them with our limblets. We feel the
Pain press against our midparts. The void that supports
our body feels cold and slippery; the void that supports
our mind is up there, in nothing; it feels like nothing.
Thought feels like nothing unless filled with something, I
think; a Feeling is something to fill it with. Our relation
to the void, is it nothing, or perhaps filled by us? Are we
a Feeling in our relation to the void?

If only, we think, there was a way to secure our items to
keep them from spilling out of us; to free all our limbs
and limblets to never feel anything such as the Pain we
felt once passed, for it was everything.

The voidlings have once again returned and we mark them as
such and continue to kick. Many fall apart, none make noise
like the one we knew when we heard it in the void once
passed. Parts of the voidlings are wet, but not all. We can
now reach down with the extension of our limbs and limblets
and Feel the something of these voidlings; it is not Pain,
which is always present, but something else. We feel the
wetness of the voidlings upon our limblets; we can rub
this wetness. We take it now—there is a voidling beneath
our limbs as we walk forward upon the void that supports
our body—it feels wet. We spread this wetness from the
voidling on our limbs. We reach toward the voidling again
and encounter items like our own; wet little bundles of
items like our own, expanding from the voidling, spilling
out onto the void that supports our body. They are cold and
wet—we feel it—and again the ideas become filled with
something. Remnants of a life once lived, we think. Where
this idea comes from escapes us, but it's ever present in
its familiarity.

We expand our limblets upon the voidlings, in search of
something—a Thought we have. We follow the wetness into
little voids inside the voidlings, like our own void, from
whence our items spilled. The thought we have is not there,
so our limbs and limblets continue expanding across the
voidlings—pain up above—until we come across something.
We feel something that is unlike the wetness of the void
that supports our body, something too unlike the wetness
and Cold of the little voidlings themselves. We feel
something that is neither Wet nor Cold nor Pain nor Thought
nor nothing. It is something that the voidling is inside,
or something to keep it from spilling out into the void
anew perhaps.

With our limblets we grasp this something, which is neither
Wet nor Cold nor Pain nor Thought nor nothing. We gather
it up with our limblets and like the void once passed when
our limb and limblets were lodglings begin tearing it from
the voidling; it is a tear—not a crack—that sets it free.
All at once this noise brings this Thought our limblets
have, forth from the voidling into our limbs. We fondle it
amidst our limblets: it is neither Cold nor Wet nor Thought
nor Pain nor Nothing, but it is something; something like
warmth; or no, perhaps more not. We have nothing but the
Thought to compare it to, which is of course something
other than the void; something to be filled yes. A void
to be filled. Little by little less of a void more of a
Thought; an item unto itself, or so it seems. But, this
something, it is more so something than anything else
because as we fondle it amidst our limblets we Thought it
can contain our items, ensuring that never again will our
limbs falter and our ideas fall down upon our heads and
leave us scattered haphazardly upon the ground.

So our limblets cease to fondle and now we take this item,
some thing we've torn from the little voidling with our
limb and limblets, and I carefully wrap it around the
section of something in our relation to the nothing of the
void that supports our body and the void that supports our
mind; we wrap it to contain the items which we've been
holding inside our personal void with our limblets to keep
them from ever again spilling out again and forcing us to
feel such terrifying things, when Pain becomes everything,
devouring the void.

Before resuming our procession, we desire to extract
another item from this life once lived. We reach deeply
into it until our limblets encounter the items like our
own. We take hold of them, extract them from the cold
little nothing. As we pull, a squelch echoes out into
the void. We pull and there seems to be no end to it.
Our limblets wet with something cold and sticky. The item
extracted we coil nicely on the void that supports our
body, nearby. These items, we think, can be studied at a
later time. Perhaps there is a meaning we can extract from
them. Finally we reach an end to what we hold in our hands.
There is a slight resistance, not much. It's easy to tear
it out of the voidling and complete the coiled item resting
next to us.

Again we reach inside this little life once lived, that
refuses to crumble, at least for now. What do we find?
More items that seem familiar to the touch. Perhaps once
before we extracted items from voidlings for a living, to
be reused for some other purpose before they too, crumbled
apart like many of the ones found in the void once passed.
After collecting as many as the softer ones as we can and
piling them nearby, we get to work on the harder ones, the
items of more resistance. With our limbs and limblets, we
pry these items apart. Many crack as they're extracted.
It's as if they might be bones. Yes, we remember something
distant. There was once a time where we encountered
something like we are now. Or pehaps engineered it. A
small mound of bones, one placed atop the other. Our ideas
escape us once again. But is it not what we desired in our
extraction: some other Thought to fill the void?

A momentary Feeling of a life once lived.

Feeling is something like a noise we know when we hear it; we know when we feel it. Feeling is full of Pain, I think; this is something that we experienced in the void once passed perhaps as well when, if there really is such a place, we were without the void, or the void as we know it now. Because again the voidlings seem like something rather than nothing, like something we knew before the emptiness of the void: something cold, our scraping wetness.

It is a construction we need to mark. For with Feeling comes Thought right behind it. For us, voided in darkness as we are, it's difficult to extract one from the other. For does feeling elicit Thought, or is it simply the result of the Feeling? We're unsure of the answer. Aren't they one in the same, we ask ourselves? Is causing a Thought the same thing as a Thought being the result of an item encountered by the tips of our limblets?

Beneath our limbs is something. We know it is cold, but why?

As if in answer, a wetness falls down from high above, from higher than where our ideas sit perched in the void that supports our mind. A drop? It drops? We're not sure if this is the right Thought, but we continue expanding this idea, to fill it up or cast it aside.

A drop onto where our ideas sit perched up above in the
nothing of the void. A drop that makes a noise we know when
we hear it. We feel it when we hear it; there is the splat,
as if something gathered up all of Feeling, Noise and Time,
and pushed them together, then tumbled them down, dropped
them down upon the void around our mind, confusing our
ideas.

This drop, this splat from the void above the void, this
is something; it too is a wetness much like the one from
the void moments passed. I mark it as such. Then again,
another splat. We feel a wetness from the point the
splat has dropped down upon our ideas in the void that
supports our mind and it travels inchwards, cold and wet,
expanding, being pulled toward limb then limblet. Perhaps
they continue down onto the void that supports our body,
although in this way they cannot be properly marked,
forcefully pulled as they are from the void above the void
above that supports our mind.

This is also a feeling, I believe. Rain is what we feel
fall down upon us—it is rain—that's something we're
sure of now. Screaming into the void the rain that splats
upon our limbs and limblets, it answers: it is something
we felt from before the void, so far away from nothing. We
remember water falling into water and the sound it made.
One of our limbs aches with the Thought of it. The way it
travels and collects.

But what is it? It is changing. The splats gather in great
heaps, gather into themselves, the heaps of splats of rain.
I'm expanding into them with my limblets, trying to gather

them as items, into themselves—but the heaps of splats
of rain refuse to follow. The rain is part of something,
even now, we think. I can almost bring them above with my
limblets, the splats pouring inchwards from the void above
the void above.

We expand our limbs, scraping with force into the moistness
that now supports us. In place of the frozen Pain that was
once the void that supports our body, is something we can
almost taste. It is doing something to us, we think; more
and more, each time it wets our limblets. We are getting
closer. The ideas are dancing above in time with the splats
which drip down upon our limblets. It's something I can
almost recognize, the splats, the noise they make now,
when we hear them tumble inchwards towards the void that
supports our body, now forever changed. This is not Pain,
but something else entirely. Not quite Pain nor Thought
nor Cold nor Wet—it is Wet, but that's not all—nor the
void nor nothing nor Feeling. It is Memory, we think. The
pull of historic items. We haven't always been here. Or
this reality—voidspace—perhaps, is better. The void is
an enemy of times once passed. It feels like the void that
exists above, below, out beyond our reach, is located
within, consciously shrouding the essence of what we once
were.

These splats rain down upon me for moments Time and I can
never mark, but we are content to try to mark them into
something anyways, for we know they are. Pain has begun
again to nudge its way into our thoughts and although we
remain still in our relation to the void, it is everpresent
now, timing in throb with the splats and gathering wetness
about our cold limbs; cold from lack of expansion? From

the wetness of the splats perhaps. We stretch our limbs out
upon the void that supports our body, which is now covered
in bundles of splats of rain we cannot gather, although we
continue to try, drawing forth our limblets, expanding them
into the wetness, searching for something we forgot.

The noise it makes is comforting to us in its familiarity
and we forget, only for a moment, our vacuous
circumstances.

We remained pressed amidst the splats that fell from the
void above until they ceased. Perhaps we slipped into
nothing again, for there was a moment the splats rained
down upon us, and Time had ceased to mark, for they were
many. Something much more than one.

Time then marked their ceasing by crashing down upon where
we remained in our relation to the void, pressed flat. Now
it more or less resembles the void once passed, although
evidence of the splats of rain remain pressed into it,
marks unto themselves.

With great effort we force our limbs to expand, raising
our ideas up towards the void above, pushing our limbs
and limblets outwards until again we feel the precise
separation of the void that supports our body and the
void that supports our mind. It' s nothing, I think. What
was once the void passed, the void with splatlets, is now
nothing again. Not quite nothing—an idea, a Memory we' ve
made—but something mostly unchanged, slightly not nothing,
or not the nothing we knew before our expansion outward
into the void. There is something up above, something close
by that we cannot reach. Perhaps it' s nothing. For the
moment Pain is nowhere to be found.

What else is there? What else can we do with our limblets,
which seem to be something created for expanding, even if
it' s into nothing: a Feeling perhaps, nothing more. Like
the voidlings beneath our limbs, scraping away on the cold
void below, the somethings are becoming easier to mark;
easier, in Time, for our thoughts are becoming filled with
items to return to, empty or not. Perhaps this returning

is something to mark. This opposite of expanding outwards,
pulling thoughts, like items, together, drawing inwards
like the items once clutched with limblets.

This opposite of expanding outwards is an idea perhaps.

The opposite of expanding outwards into the void is like
the way once passed when we put our items back; limb and
limblets scraped to gather and place them back inside our
personal void, our squelching midparts once spilled. They
were much like the items we coiled upon the cold voided
ground once passed in our exploration of the little life
once lived, the voidling that resisted crumbling beneath
our grasp.

We have created something out of nothing by collecting ideas,
or marking things in Time, as our progression into the void
expands. This seems strange, as if something is developing;
once we began our expansion out into the nothing of the void,
eternity began becoming somewhat smaller; we found ourselves
more able to fit inside certain items. No, not that: we found
these ideas are not quite hindrances at all. This is closer,
I think. The ideas, standing on themselves, want to say
something; they want to tell us of times before the void, but
cannot.

For they present themselves in ways we' ve yet to learn.
They are inarticulate. But they remain, and this alone is
something to mark. Are they Feeling, or Memory? Perhaps both
or neither. A life once lived. What is a life once lived?
Something from the void once passed or something else? Another
creature stumbling aimlessly through nothing. As we progress,
continue our expansion, our limbs flex and Feel for something
familiar. We begin to realize that each part of us is slightly
different. Our limbs are unique. Upon inspection, their
contours mismatched. One warm, one cold, and the other, slick
with something unidentifiable. It' s as if we were pieced
together from discarded parts, powerful items, but wholly
different.

Ideas stand on top of each other, or mix inwards; although we
can' t be sure, it seems since our expansion into the void,
perhaps we, or I as well, are expanding; our ideas, limbs,
even the voided midparts and items are all things that at one
point—before we stretched out our limbs and limblets into
the emptiness of the void—did not exist, or did so unmarked,
as it were once passed.

Is this history?

We draw our ideas inward now, into ourselves, to focus on the
time in the void once passed we encountered the voidling that
was different from the others; the one with which we shared
our Pain.

Now more than ever, I think, we are sure that our relation
to the void—this nothing we were peopled in—has something
to do with these voidlings, which we are crushing even now
beneath our limbs tracing the bundles of splatlets in our
progression out into the void anew.

The voidlings. Perhaps, should we encounter more like the
previous one, we will hesitate to press upon it with limb and
limblet until we have time to to study it.

But now, as we press outwards, inching onwards amidst the damp
splats and crumbling voidlings we feel nothing new; only the
cold, damp scruff beneath our limbs as it breaks apart.

I'm not sure, but Pain, we think, has begun to present
itself again, as if something of the moment has given it
embodiment; perhaps the lack of new things makes our thoughts
turn inwards, to Pain once more, our items pressed behind the
thing we ripped from the voidling to prevent their spillage.

To pass the Time—this is something we know has been said before; some fish to pass the time. To pass the Time we focus on the sound of limb and limblet scraping inchwards on the splatlets and the voidlings beneath. It is something that seems like nothing at first; only after a Time do we realize that this is something new to think about: a sound we know when we hear it, the scraping and the splatlets and the crumblings of the matter beneath us; beneath our limbs and ideas. Is it ground? Are we grounded? Our ideas are not, for they float well above the space where our limbs and limblets mesh with the cold thresh of voidlings. But what about this; where our body is supported. We are a body? I try to remember how this could be, how maybe we are the same as the voidlings, how they break apart beneath our limbs; but what they once were, was it something?

Our thoughts all tumble and dance, as if to taste the splatlets bundled together on what we will for now call the ground, for two voids and all these ideas have become nearly overwhelming. There is only one void, I think, and it is nothing, but it has so many somethings now; including— we agree—a ground upon which we rest our limbs and limblets; part of them anyways; and then upon which, as we stop to listen, a phwwwwwwww or a whsssssshhhhh, a sound we at once both hear and feel. Or perhaps it is a feeling we hear, and a sound we feel. Something to get excited about? Certainly one to mark as such, feeling and hearing and hearing and feeling this new item, which at once grows louder as we absorb this idea, the fullest yet, we think; something we can mark as so far away from nothing it is like nothing we've ever known before. One of our limbs seems to react in a strange way to the noise, it tingles in a manner unfelt before, as if for a moment part of it is trying to escape from our body. As if the exterior of this limb has been frozen and is now thawing out.

We begin our procession once again—expanding outwards with our limblets—when we hear another Feeling that sounds like Crack; this we've once marked, and know it as such. We can hearfeel its expansion; it's all around us now, above where our ideas flow and beneath, on the ground where our limbs rest amidst the voidlings.

The crack cracks and then cracks again, while the soundfeeling continues to grow. After a time there are no more cracks and the soundfeeling subsides, and we continue pressing out into nothing, with an ever-growing band of somethings floating above our head: evidence, items once marked, Thought, Pain, Feeling, Cold, Ideas; until suddenly we're hindered— ceased—by something quite unlike nothing we're used to, either marked previously or expanded into ideas, ceasing our progression entirely.

There is the ground, the void once passed, the void wherefloats our ideas, and the void which we expand through, which is now blocked.

The blockage does not crumble to the touch, unlike the little voidlings. We scrape against it with our limblets, and so it scrapes; we hear this noise and when we hear it, we know how it feels. We feel and hear to the touch at the same time. Because this hindrance can be touched. And we reach out to it, to feel its scraping feeling; to see if Time might have made a mistake; to see if there is one, and then the other—the feeling then the sound—or if they're an item.

We scrape it frontways until our limblets throb; until the
limblets on our other limb begin to throb as well. Here's
something, I think to myself, proffering askance unto the
void. I place my question to the air, to see if something
offers a reply; at first, I am unable to articulate it;
instead I scream out into the air. I am unable to formulate
anything but nonsense; we have been defeated, in an effort to
communicate something to nothing. We scoff, then continue to
scrape inchwards into the item which blocks our path.

But the new thing—forgive us—we've forgotten in our
attempt to manage our ideas above and the feelings below and
the throb from our moistened midparts—this hindrance, it is
trying to tell us something; something aside from nothing;
something in connection to everything; or everything that's
now happened. Because there is the scrape and the feeling, or
rather the feeling and the sound as a result of the scrape
of our limblets in their relationship to the hindrance in
the void; there is this—which occurs in Time—then there is
something slightly afterwards, which is foreign to us.

We have this: there are the voids—together only one—
separated for the convenience of our ideas such that one
floats above our head, while the other supports our body;
in other words, the void once passed and our expansion
frontwards, now blocked by the hindrance. We scrape the
hindrance with our limblets and experience a Feeling and a
Noise as one, then shortly afterwards a strange sensation; or
rather a thickness in the void that supports our mind; perhaps
not a thickness, rather, but a thickening, as if for a brief
moment that area around our ideas begins to have some sort of
different, indescribable quality: a Sensation, I think, much
like Feeling although quite different from Feeling, or what

we can scrape with limb and limblet. We scratch, then feel and hear; then the sensations make our ideas shudder; and then we hear a sniff—it is a new noise—and our ideas shudder again then and our limblets seize, and we sneeze out into the void.

Pain is ever-present on the fringe, floating away in the void above our head, or tapping occasionally from the force of our limbs from where our items sit bundled up behind the cloth we've torn from the voilding once passed. We scratch and scratch. We feel and hear, press into it and fill our ideas with something new; some sort of piney something. A smell perhaps— something we are reminded of just then—a smell is something far from nothing. A snout to pick out smells from the air. There were smells once. We recognize this one before us. Somewhere deep inside of us a Memory sits holding a scent, a meaning waiting to be extracted, unlocked, and lived perhaps, once again, a fleeting means of escape.

Inspired, we scream and press our limbs with force into the hindrance. We Hear and Feel nothing but a slight throb in our insides. We scream again and pull our ideas inchwards toward us and with everything push again into the item. This time it cracks, causing us to push harder, then cracks again, then a kind of whoosh like air.

Still we stay, to listen for something; to see if there are
items to be felt, or anything at all. Our limbs relax only
for a moment, because no sooner had we begun again to feel
the crunch of voidlings crumble on the ground beneath our
limbs than we are ceased by another hindrance; all it takes
to unlock this idea is the scrape of bark upon our snout.
And again, the piney smell of a forest rising somewhere in
the darkness in front of us. Our limbs scraped the broken
needles beneath hooves and in a heartbeat we're trading
the void for air; the lack of everything for light and
motion.

Surrounding us are others like we once were, before the
hunt caught up with us. The sulfuric smell that rents
the air. A memory of when they cut up the ancient one;
the horned ancient one they cut, they tore him apart with
the smell in the air. A life once lived now lived again.
Unlocked inside of us. Puzzled out into the forest.

We remember it; all of us remember there was first: the
smell, then we saw what the smell did to him—it was sour—
we saw him split in half, his life and horns hung all
apart from him in layers. So now we run, with the smell
not far behind, burning our senses, filling the air with
fear. We run since how we've always run, since before
we can remember we have learned how to run. We are born
running, albeit some on shaky legs, we are born running
before any of us grow spots to tell us apart. Perhaps there
have always been spotless children running from a smell in
the dark. Or the smell of something has been chasing us
always—that could be so—but now the green pisses by our
ears as we run for fear of splitting apart into pieces.
The air cracks with the sound of the smell as it whizzes

by our peaked ears, which quiver each time the sour smell
comes close to us. We scrape our way through the forest
with our cloven hoofs, clutching the mud between our steps
like we' ve been taught since before we were born. We are
all of us, as one, expanding out into the forest for fear
of blowing apart into pieces. The sound whizzes by our
ears once again and one of the trees now appearing in the
void nearby explodes, showering us with splintered bark,
insides spilling out into the forest to be trampled by our
hooves; perhaps as well by the makers of the sour noise
which follows. When we were young the dew was fresh upon
our lips, the grass soft and pliant. Pliant like the wind
brushing our ears at night; something to be moved through,
the wind. We are moving through it now, or it through
us, tickling our midparts as the hum from our tramplings
intensifies. The noise is never far away. Even at night we
now hear, close to our beds of leaves. It wakes us with
a start early when the dew is fresh and then we begin to
run. As always, since we remember, running, moving ever
outward into the forest. The ancient one said before he
disappeared that the forest was not everything, that
there was something beyond it. But we' ve been expanding
throughout it since what seems like ages and none of us
have ever reached anything but green. It is painful for
us to run from the hunters, from the sound that cracks
the air, that burns our eyes and nostrils in the dusk and
early morning. For some days it seems that we must never
stop running, and so we continue, expanding outwards into
the green above and the green below. Our hooves scrape us
inch by inch further into the darkness, the canopy guards
our thoughts, broken open by the cracking rent of the sour
smell. Once we came upon a dark place, with mud as thick
as our hooves themselves, or so it seemed, for we sunk so
far down. This dark place, peopled with trees of gaseous
green, dark green, fur hanging down like the beards of

witches from stories of the forest once passed the ancient
one handed us before he fell to pieces, his items spilled
fresh upon the forest floor. In the dark place once was
a smell like this, like the one chasing us now. A sour
smell. Something from somewhere long ago, or returning to
something we could never reach. Some land where everything
sinks. Something of that sort follows us now, as we make
our way with the trees above, crunching a path through the
twigs and branches scattered upon the forest floor; we kick
them with our hooves, we scatter the items beneath us in
our race outwards, a life once lived seeking a place to
rest, something far away from the sound that stalks us now.

Once we think we saw something of the smell, the producer
perhaps, but when we realized what it was something
happened to our eyes and it was already gone. Eaten again
into darkness. They stood on their back two legs, covered
in colors like the rotting place before. It was there
they were and then they weren' t; we paused briefly, then
stretched our limbs out beneath us, running as fast as
we could for fear of blowing apart like our elders or
the nearby trees. We felt the pain when the horns of the
ancient one were cut away by those we cannot see, the
makers of the sulfurous smell which rents the air: the
hunters. The old ones fall for they have not the heart to
press their hooves into the ground and use the wind to
guide them forward. We now carve our way deeper into the
green while the trees piss by our softened ears due to
youth, but age draws deeper upon us, ever inwards, becoming
heavier and heavier.

Eventually we no longer bound about as freely; the sour
smell catches you then, and pulls away your bark until you

heat the forest floor with death. As if in reply a tree
shatters close by our heads and the herd must bound back
then around away from danger; our ears always point toward
where the hunters, unseen, travel, unhinged by fear but
running all the same, to spread out and fall upon us when
they catch us out of the air and onto the floor, spill our
life out and cut our antlers away. We have never seen this,
but somewhere inwards we feel the pain of our ancients,
collective stories of how they cut our power from us, our
points we feed to the wind, the points we use to protect
ourselves and challenge outsiders; these are removed and
placed elsewhere in dishonor. The air carries the thousand
pointed memories of pain, a void of distant tramplings upon
the forest ground; the tramplings then the end of running:
death. When our old one lost his points it was as if air
became water; we floated for a moment then sunk. When
the power of the pointed limbs subsided, we quivered and
screamed and our knees bent backwards and understood that
eventually, we would be that happening. Perhaps one or all
of us. But when we die, we offer our agelong journey to the
air to be used for we know not what.

There is a looming prescence, a memory of darkness,
following the hunters in their chase, but it seems unreal,
distant. We're unable to determine if it's meant for us,
or them. The herd is proceeding deeper. The smellnoise no
longer follows us for a time but it will return, forcing
us to renew our procession deeper into the vegetative
gloom. For the farther we travel the more the forest falls
apart beneath our limbs; the leaves become less pliant;
the detritus of ancient elms and weeping foliage tell us
the herd has travelled too far, that we've entered the
death place. We run faster, to try to find something beyond
this, something further than death: a land past death,

where we'll be carried by the power of our points, our
ancient stories propelling us out into nothing, then beyond
it, again, to taste of something different, to escape the
cycle. We've been running since before we can remember;
no, back in our history we were held in darkness, then
escaped. We extracted freedom by forcing the forest to
open up in front of us. Now the smell is overpowering. The
sulfuric stench which rents the air—the hunters death
machines—leaves a fear eating away at the our collected
stories, the ones that gave us life. Nothing compares. We
run our hooves into pieces of beaten meat to escape such
sciences.

But we remember items from the forest once passed, when
the dew fell fresh upon the pliant grass we munched at
leisure, free from fear. Our herd felt nothing but joy.
The wind lifted us up without askance and kept us bouyant
until we tired. Always the green of the forest pissing by,
blurred into one color. We smelled urine on the air and
knew where it was to mark, and where were marks already. In
heat, we breathed in mates that made our mouths water, so
we lapped up water too, and spit it out on whatever trunk
we pleased. Things did not explode so easily. The items of
ourselves stayed inside as they were made to, and the items
of the forest aided us as they could. The trees held the
branches and the herd kept track of the months by focusing
intimately on the color of the leaves. We felt bark crumble
away beneath our rumps. Fear always elsewhere, in the deep
rotten woods in which we find ourselves now; the woods
beyond the forest, beyond everything that once was passed;
beyond everything that was nothing; the ancient one' s
moldy bones, a monument unanswered. Piled by the stream in
a nest of ferns unfolding, for what are bones gathering
moss if not a soul passes to see them?

They are nothing.

We continue deeper, with the smell pissing by our ears.
There is no time now. We are forever running, from death
as the hunters, chosen to return us to nothing; the void
edges slowly around our vision, inescapable even still.
There must be many hunters, mixed together with the smell
of leaves. No. We are wrong. They have tricked us. It's
not leaves we smell oh how they rot, but not leaves. It's
the musk of our dead. The flavors of a life once lived. Our
loved ones. They drive us forward in a frenzy, pushing us
into a horde, making us horny with death; the death of our
loved ones—ones forgotten until now—as our nostrils flood
with the smell of their sex. The forest, the smell. Death
hunters using them against us. They're using them against
us as weapons to drive us forward into unsafe areas, into
places where neither hold nor hoof can find purchase amidst
the sinking rotten forest. Things are dead. Even the things
that are living are dead and the air becomes heavier,
harder to breathe and fly through. Though perhaps our limbs
are culprits; our limbs carry us into the air, but they
cannot continue. We haven't even time to rest. Perhaps it
is all of us heavy, our spirits flag. Driven ever forward,
being pressed back into inexplicable darkness.

I hear one of us howling. I can smell their death. They've
been pounced upon by the sour smell. Even now our nostrils
burn with it, our ears ring. If we have been running since
forever, perhaps it has always been behind us. Perhaps
there is nothing but nothing but the chase. Is this now?
Perhaps we haven't ever stopped running. Perhaps what's
here before us is only memory. But we never stop pushing
into the mud squeezing toes wiped off on the next step
punched through beds of leaves. Are we a spectator or
part of the herd? We barely have time to wonder, scraping
forward as the forest disappears, the spent smell of sex,

of death looming after us like black fire. The smell rents
the air amidst our flight and we think again we've heard
the call of our brother fallen among the rotting ground but
there's no pause—no hesitation—for the piss of death
travels between our toes, pricking up our mane of spiny
digits.

————Where we are now we have never been. Where we have never

been we are never going. We are never going anywhere but

here, for here is where we'll always remain————

Time is dragging along behind us, or perhaps woven around
our necks. Where is it from, and when will it stop hurting
us?

How long has the herd been running only to escape back into
nothing?

Now we live more in the air than on the ground. Death
follows us everywhere we go; in the forest, it is like our
grandfather. When will it tire of the chase? Where will it
drop us when it does?

——A piece of metal has burnt its way into my chest ——

A piece of metal—the smell—a bullet has burnt its way
into my chest. Or something. The forest has burnt its way
into my life. No. Something has pissed its breath into my
lungs. Perhaps. Now hit the ground with a thud and they
trampled me. Who could blame them. Hit the ground with a
thud traced hooves into my snout, my muzzle side whole
body, punched-through flesh. The frenzy. Trampled me, who
could blame them? Far off the forest melts behind them;
leaves scatter something. I sink into the ground. We are
returning. My limbs thrust forward. I place them. Hooves.
Find little purchase in the rotten muck. We persist, find
the foothold and lift. Unsure we chatter our bones together
and collapse. Our backwards knees. It isn' t good. The
forest enemy. We raise ourselves. We slip, the forest finds
us on its rotten floor again: the vegetal leaves that smell
so close to sour but not yet quite. We feel ourselves
being dragged into something. Or slipping. Slipping? No.
Spilling. Escaping. Voiding ourselves. Voiding outwards. In
the forest long ago before moss upon the bones of ancient
the air running born we are alone. We were never running
really. Or were we always? Where did we come from and why
are we here, now? Born in the air. Sinking into death the
forest floor. It wraps its vegetal glow surrounds us. We
hear far off the smells rent the air. Far off where our
others run, the air struggles to heave them up. Perhaps
the forest thins where the herd runs now. No? Perhaps
it is I who will help them escape. All slowing I move
myself further into the trees. I will draw them to me,
the hunters. I scrape at the ground in progress. Far off
something like night, edging in to make it fade. Receding.
The trees no longer beautiful but terrifying. Stripped of
necessity: barren, charred. We have been successful in
making it this far. Huddle now. Make it to the edge of
nothing, no. Make it behind an area in the ground. The
ground is sinking. We are falling away from the forest.

It's looming now, darkness. It is dark where we're
going; dark perhaps where we've been. Dew a remembrance:
something one can simply smell and feel at home. If only.
I cry but bubbles away my throat like the farting ground.
There was a place in my neck where meaning once stood. The
forest, the smell; it all at once overcomes our spirit.
Will we remember this, once death consumes us? The forest,
the smell. The hunt like it was. Forever. The hunt forever
running, chasing into air. They will fall upon me then. The
hunt. The makers of flight. For us? Perhaps they are the
reason always running. The smell rents the air. Blowing
apart the bark of those that live inside us. Our sisters
born. Our brothers born. Blown apart eventually, when the
air refuses them. Heavy we sink taken down, the vegetal
state of our bodies. For when we stop running we die. Or
no? When will we die I am dying. The stagnant water fills
my hoof prints, tracing a trail back to when the dew was
sweet. Back to the days we were a part of once. We were
born into the pack, we think. How did we make it this far?
If there was ever a place to run it is backwards, not
forwards. Perhaps they've found the place where the forest
ends. There are stones there many colored; so said the
ancient one—our guide—before the hunt hacked his storied
greatness into moss. Left upon the ground, grown green not
bleach the sun forever divided upon the forest floor. We
have worn our life apart. Pull the bark and sniff the sap;
may it pay for us. The hunt comes closer. Twigs beneath.
Twigs the forest floor. We lift ourselves up, head then
neck then body then limb; we hardly can tell from life
painting sodden ground below, our life once red when the
sun went down. The forest at night. The forest at down. The
hunt approaches; we smell their sour musk. Piss of death,
clink of iron. Leaves dead tremble the forest floor; kick
themselves closer to our death. We try to rise, slip, try
again. It's leaving us. Our stories float above our heads

in darkness. No. Our vision fails; glows. No. Comes back
now blue. Sunlight? I smell a sister in the air, one met
long ago the ground. They wear her piss to drive us mad.
I cannot away. We have prepared. Come, melt my bones with
moss; bog them up. The air bore the smell of death times
a thousand. Piss-bottled addlers. Green the dusk. Spare
nothing. Ritual. Tie coils around the heart of space. Place
us near the running water. They lift us up. Sideways.
Upside down. Our molting heads brush the forest floor.
We paint with life. The sun goes down. Our fake sisters
crunch along beside us; chatter floods our softened ears.
The air no longer cares. It' s our fault, not hers. Never
hers. Stories flood our nostrils. We remember then forget.
Our limbs. Hooves clack, tied together. The forest floor.
Antlers. No moss. No. Never did we think it could turn that
way, did we think our piss; we are covered in our piss.
It matts the fur and dribbles off our snout. The sun is
upside down. Green disappearing. Perhaps their flight has
found the edge. The hunt. Is there a flock of them or have
they fallen upon me. Beneath us they have placed an item to
catch our leakage. Powerless to snort. Slip the life out of
it, we' re ready. Come out then. Come then. Stop rustling
direction. Forward leave. Come finish it. Scraping toward
us. Sight depends on water we watch fill hoof prints; the
mud spackle. Much like hunger this feeling. Or no? And then
it comes glinting. We wish our brothers and sisters luck.
The forest, green, the smell falls upon us. We struggle to
huff and watch our breath disappear, the sun disappear, the
forest, our smell. The hunt—the knife—pierces us close by
our musky parts—a history—comes scaling down, opening us
up. Iron wets the forest floor; everything spills out. The
rotting leaves. What is this death? The smell of death. The
smell of shit.

———A fly finds a resting place upon our rump ———

Our stories float above our head. Are we what we were? Is the void what it was once passed? We are here and we are there, or not?

What was in the void once passed perhaps only Memory. It must, for we are here where we once were again, or have never left. It remains Cold. Even still, here, after our memory. Pain, Time, what else? We pause. I reach out our limbs, our limblets scrape the bark. We know that now: bark, trees, the forest; now the void.

Was it us? No.
Or perhaps something.

We expand ever outwards, aware of what's in front of us: the Idea of the Forest. When the shit hit our face.

Remembrance.
        ——The piss——
A life once lived, a death once lived.

Something to mark. But now nothing but the void. Now and perhaps always. But that was behind us, but now is with us, floating above our heads as we expand, scraping darkness, scratching bark.

Smell we recognize vegetal musk. Each item we encounter tumbles outward as we inch our way through the forest, which we see as nothing. For what else could it be.

In the void once passed we were vision, light; green and a life like red. But we have receded again. Is it still a void if it's peopled with somethings? Here, or nowhere,

but it is ours. It is meant for us to own this darkness.
Perhaps only for these ideas do we exist. To be reminded of
nothing we can explain.

Outwardly, we continue, inwardly, hindered. But even a
hindrance can be something more than nothing. Memory has
helped us—has gained us something—because we knew not
what existed in our life once lived.

Pushing trees like nothing cracked toward vegetal ground we
smell our surroundings. Where did this come from? Something
to decide. Do we decide something or is something decided
for us? Perhaps we've been prepared for this. But we are
a physical idea. There is Pain. Something aside from, also
accompanied by, Thought, Time, Memory. We Feel something.
Now again, we remember. Touch with limblets our open void,
stuffed full with once-spilled items. We remember. The pain
we remember. We move our limb to scrape at our snout. It
Feels like we remember. But the rest is all wrong.

Exploring our contours, it's as if there are only bits and
pieces of our life with the herd. A limb bent backward at
the knees. The smells which guide us. We stumble and scrape
outwards, unsteadily through the void. Things are becoming
something, we can Feel it. Understanding. We scrape,
stretch our limblets to the cold ground, extract ideas.
Pain, Memory, Time, Feeling: different now. Us.

The ground I think is not a void. It is of the void—in
the void—but, it is the ground. We think this is how it
is supposed to be. The Forest likewise. Perhaps the void
is what we imagine to exist. Perhaps these other items are
there, here, where we are, but unable to be accessed, as
if we're unable to draw them out, or can only glimpse at
some part of them. We remember the forest and for a moment,
our snout twitches. One of our limbs tingle, but only so

quickly to disappear—eaten up again into darkness—so
slight we question if it was something to mark. Our Stories
float above our head, separate from the void. Items, like
ideas, shaped by memory. Or memory, in its relation to the
void. Are we only what we are from memory? Is that what
has pieced our body together? Perhaps this is something.
For we remember our progression: our procession outwards
in relation to the void. Even before the flash back to the
void once passed when in the forest running with the others
we remember we had the idea of expanding outwards, and
then continued, until there were many things to be filled
floating above our head.

So we carry these things with us, out into nothing, which is
slowly turning into something more than what it once was,
because of these things we carry, or in spite of them. What
we kick, what we Feel with our limbs, grunt and swallow.
Smell a history. Smells once, from the forest. From the
smell the hunt the glint and sour smell still burning. It is
steeped within us now. Another Story. Another Time. We are
here, but part of us is back there, where we once were: the
wind, which carries us up into the air and back down into
nothing.

We remember darkness and the rotting leaves on the forest
floor. Perhaps they' re here with us now, as well, a
small part of nothing; or perhaps only as such because our
knowledge escapes us; a story to be remembered.

We continue forward, out of the forest now, we think.

We can no longer feel the trees hinder our progression,
but we hear traces of them upon the wind. In the void once
passed, where the wind held us up, we were something other
than we are now. Or maybe both things at once. Our keen
sight. The smells upon the air. Somewhere inside us sits
the joy of that memory, but there we cannot call it up.
We' re unable to extract it, to explore its meaning. Is
it possible to live two lives at once? We are creating a
fractured history inside ourselves—where we now know noises
and Touch and Feel and remembrance and Pain and Thought and
everything; at once nothing, just nothing, then, for some
reason, there was motion, movement, pushing outwards with
things we didn' t understand, collecting items, expanding
our ideas. We can feel us getting bigger, an inventory.

We Feel the Cold Ground. It's a Ground because we Feel it
beneath our limbs. Will it continue or are we afraid it will
drop away and leave us? Are we afraid for knowing nothing,
or that there's nothing to find, or that, perhaps, we might
find that nothing is only something we do not yet know and
which we'll be forced to piece together like our history as
another history?

We stand silent. Our ideas apart from us. The stale air
of the void is heavy like a cloak. The items we remember
inside of us, they feel like nothing. We are a fool. There
is nothing for us to learn, to understand. We think all of
these things that scrape along with us are created out of
fear, ideas to keep us comforted.

Nothing matters but the void.

We refuse to progress further until we' re sure that where
we' re going is something other than nothing.

Can we be frightened if we don' t exist?

If we exist, we can be frightened, but fear exists only
inasmuch as we allow it to. For our existence gives it
power. Our Memory. The Stories from the void once passed,
they exist as much as we do, perhaps more.

This is nothing like we' ve Thought of before. We are
unsure if it' s going forward or backward, inasmuch as
ideas are concerned. But we must continue. For if we exist,
moving forward will perhaps be the only way we can prove
such existence.

As if in answer to such thoughts, a noise is sent to us
upon the wind, drawing us toward it. We try to cease our
progression, to pause in quiet, perhaps articulate a form
of response, but find ourselves unable to cease.

We lie down, stretch out our body upon the ground, but
still we are dragged forward, scraping over whatever is in
our path, summoned towards this spectral voice. At times it
seems it' s the wind itself; others, a pained and distant
memory, an inarticulate longing we recognize as language.
Like the voidling: a life once lived. We remain powerless
to resist it, or question.

Traveling fast now, the Cold ground begins to tear at us, to shred our exterior as we increase speed, the voice upon the wind growing stronger. It is a soft sound, but one that fills us with incomparable terror. A sound as familiar as Death. Where are our memories now? We struggle to call upon them, to extract anything, bits and pieces or another answer that might help us discover its purpose—the noise—an item we can use in case of danger. But our memories fail us. The only recognition granted us is a strange familiarity with the timbre of the summoning wind.

It is growing louder now—louder still—as we' re torn across the Cold and jagged Ground. We realize we are screaming. The noise draws us ever forward. Deafening though our screams are, they cannot compete with the resonant sound of the chant upon the wind, the soft and penetrating hum that calls us toward it. We are almost there. Our entire being is vibrating violently. All our limbs go taught. No longer able to resist, we are dragged into the circle.

We are trapped, unable to continue our progression through
the void. Something has drawn us away from our path and
now, we struggle against these walls, which have imprisoned
us. The sound has stopped momentarily. The only noise we
can hear is the Wind, brushing through the Forest in the
distance. Could it be it was only that; but no, there is a
noise nearby. One familiar. Something is breathing. We can
feel the warmth of breath upon us, as though it's many
times larger than ourselves. It is a calm and steady noise.
We scream in protest, but the pace and depth of breathing
remains unchanged, it terrifies us.

Do you know where you are? Can you speak?

Like the voidling once passed, the other life once lived,
it utters nonsense. Noises we're unable to identify. A
space inside us exists that can almost understand, but not
quite. We cannot articulate. Our answers come in huffs and
gurgles, bubbling out into nothing. We try to escape our
barrier by climbing upwards and scratching the ground with
our limbs, but it is useless. The noise has built a wall
surrounding us, such great power.

Answer me, can you speak?

The noise pauses, inhales deeply then screams into the
void. We do so as well, seeing it as the only way we can
show this power that we too, are of the void; that there is
something in common for us to explore. After the screaming
subsides, we are met once again with steady, short breaths,
the smell almost a sweetness to us.

You haven' t language yet have you? That' s alright. You will. Then you can remember this moment, this memory, and you will better understand. Or perhaps not. It is of little importance to me whether you grasp the meaning of this or remain aloof. Either way, you' ll serve me.

We lunge at the noise nearby and hit the wall in front of us forcefully, feeling the same violent vibration from a moment passed.

It is of no use, you cannot break it...

The being, or noise, or entity in front of us draws in
another deep breath.

*For your sake, I hope that you can extract meaning from
this moment. There will be no others like it for an
eternity. Until many things have passed. Until this burning
world reverts to ice. Can you see? Have you seen your
surroundings; what you trudge through and pass; what lays
upon the frosted banks?*

We grunt and burble, scraping the ground with our limblets
to test the length of our prison, its dimensions. There is
little room for much else.

*There are many working parts to the machinery of the
cosmos, and although I know not why, you have wedged your
way into its spokes. You have something to fulfill that's
inescapable, for both failure and success results in total
annihilation. I have spoken your name upon the wind to give
you meaning.*

The being begins chanting in a voice no louder than a
whisper, it is rythmic, but uninteligible to us. As the
voice continues, growing in volume, increasing rapidly in
repetition, we begin to feel our body being lifted into
the air. Our limbs vibrating like the fire of the sun.
We realize we are again screaming in Pain, in terror,
the chant now being shouted upon the wind but in our

madness, we're unable to determine its meaning; a series
of unintelligible exclamations, but each time a word is
said, our entire body feels as if a block of wood has
been hammered into it. It touches our limbs one by one,
penetrating our knees, bending our limbs backwards. It
enters our midparts, forcing a burning hole through our
chest. The last word, screamed over and over again, shoots
into our memories. We glimpse the fractured heartbeat of a
child; a face, soft and pale with piercing black eyes, then
the body of the face running in an impenetrable expanse of
whiteness. We drop back upon the ground with with a hard
thud.

—— Then there is nothing ——

We awake with a singular image in our mind amidst a
multitude of questions unanswered. The void has reopened
itself again. We are kept at bay no longer. The force
hindering us has receded back into nothing. But the noise—
the voice—has left us with ideas, memories, dangling in
the air in front of us, just out of grasp. One thing we' re
certain of is that we, the voidlings and the image we were
left with have something in common. Precisely what, it begs
to be asked, to be explored.

Frantically we reach with limb and limblet to the cold
ground, in search of understanding, some sort of conference
with the portrait now burned upon our insides. We must
find a life once lived that refuses to crumble beneath our
grasp, an item that remains intact, a voidling able to be
explored. We need to read the contours of its outlines with
the tips of our limblets to form a picture matching the one
we' ve been left with, to forcefully extract its meaning.

We scrape amidst the voidlings. The spongy little lives
once lived, shaping them softly beneath our limbs;
inexplicable memories forever floating, molded into
significance—floating above—with remaining room to
be filled by something more, some space like nothing,
expanding outwards. Can we trust what' s been given to us,
the images that bubble up from somewhere inside? Were we
once what the disembodied voice showed us, a beating ball
of red grown into the running in a vast expanse, frozen in
motion like the blur blown by our ears in the forest?

Perhaps the voidlings are the hunted and we have broken
them apart in our memory.

Where does the meaning lie in us; constructing it out
of fear to forever expand forward or backward without

knowing, in search of answers we'll eventually create.
The voice upon the wind left us with just enough to
distrust ourselves. Frustrated, we continue scratching at
the ground, searching for an answer rather than one that
squirms to pieces.

We can smell the voidlings now. They are as of death, like
shit poured upon our face. They are made of shit. No. They
are hunted. Some are wet like drops of rain and others
warm; still others cold, endless. Like a forest. A forest
of the hunted. Of the dead falling apart between our frosty
digits, like nothing. Into nothing. If they exist, we exist
together in this dark place. We hear the wind of the forest
in the distance of our memory. The voidlings, were they
once like we are? If so, our existence is solidified. The
smell urges my snout to run away.

Are we a voidling or the voice we once met?

*I have spoken your name upon the wind to give you meaning
once again.*

We have placed our entire body upon the ground to seek conference with the voidlings. We are accustomed—even reveling in their overpowering stench. If our existence persists full of the passage ripened by ideas, perhaps we can create one that will force these crumbled pieces back into existence, or label them as something more than what they remain to be before us.

We crawl forward, searching for one more intact than the others.

We touch what's now in front of us: cold, stiff and unmoving, but refusing to break apart. We stretch our precious digits, the little items protruding from our limbs; we scrape them toward what's in front of us and truly feel it for the very first time. We relish recording its contours into an idea above our heads and filling Thought with Feeling.

We run our limblets up and down. Up and down. Feeling it
inside of us, a part of us, for the first time some sense
of kinship, recognition. Feeling something we somehow know
and understand. Although it still slightly eludes us.
We're certain it's similar to the voice upon the wind. It
is our primary vision now, inside our head. Outside of the
void, but inside of us.

Our limblets smooth over it, expand. We feel more inside
of us than outwards. It expands from within ourselves; not
above, where sits the others we've filled. But it fills
us, no? What remembrance. What Feeling this something new.
Running limblets up and down, our frigid digits drawing
its contours in our mind, our memories, a subtle reference
point for when we might need to draw it out again.

The little life once lived, it warms us. Inside of us
is something like our feeling from the Forest. A marked
similarity. Time swoops down and pecks freshly upon us once
again. Feeling is something shaped by memory. Experience.

Up and down, forward and back. From the fuzz to the tips
of its extremities. Frontwards backwards sidewards inwards
outwards we explore the voidling as something to be marked;
touched and invaded. Our digits invade the little voids
of the voidling. Spaces between limbs we fill with digits
until the void is filled. We pull them out and put them
in. We pull them out and run ourselves along its softened
contours, expanding. Sparking our insides with feeling. The
tufts of hair, the scratchy mounds from deep within our
Memory. The more we scrape it—understand its items—the
more we sluice with remembrance.

We compare each of its limbs to ours. They are remarkably
different, but familiar. At one time, we surmise, we were
a voidling ourselves, before becoming something out of
nothing.

We continue our exploration of its contours, invading its
empty spaces with our digits. It overwhelms us. Time,
Memory, Feeling, Thought, Pain, The Forest, Cold, The
Smell, The Hunt, The Void. They all exist inside ourself,
as well as inside the voidling. Of the Void, of nothing
and everything; a part of all we' ve created—ideas swoop
and shape—pecking everything we' ve pushed into something
else. We feel our digits in its holes and a warmth grows
within us. We scream and it responds with movement. We
rub its contours with our digits. We fill its voids with
limblets and let them spill in, out, in, out of empty
spaces; it is pulsing, tightening around us as we enter and
exit its emptiness.

The voidling begins to scream. We scream. It screams. We
feel a resistance to our exploration; we force our limbs
back inside to feel it pulse; to us this is everything. Our
warmth becomes livid. We surge our digits into the little
life once lived and again it tries to hinder us. We scream.
It screams and moves rapidly, scratching outwards, tearing
at our exterior. Unvexed, we continue exploring the pulse
of its empty spaces, further shaping our understanding.
It is not a true representative of the image burned into
our thoughts by the voice upon the wind. Nonetheless, it
too has something to tell us. It continues tearing at our
exterior, picking away little pieces of us here and there.
It reaches our midparts, removing the barrier we placed
there to hinder the spillage of our items. Now it requires

control, our digits halt its expanding limbs, which are
pushing into the air in attack. We pull one forcefully
towards us and much to our surprise, it crumbles and tears
away from the voidling; its screams travel through us,
reaching deep into our interior. The ground is now wet with
something we smelled in a memory, the iron in the Forest.
We position our limb to halt the movement of its other
limbs, pressing it upon the Ground until its resistance
recedes into nothing. We leave ourselves pressed hard upon
the voidling. It no longer moves, or pulses or pushes or
screams. Resting ourselves against its contours, the warm
wetness freezes to the ground, and Time no longer marks,
living off our warmth somewhere inside. But even now, the
vision remains.

We walk we walk we squish we stomp we inch outwards into nothing as our ideas hover in conference in the void above; between the void above the void above and our voided limblets once spilled. We walk and kick and squish and push ever outwards, into nothing, encountering nothing now for quite some time.

We walk and squish and push and step and dig our limblets into the ground, which is softening now; voidlings becoming less and less. The Ground reminds us of the space our cloven memories clacked once in the puddles whence the shit hit our face. We stumble, and for a moment, are absorbed into Memory; enveloped by what has once passed when the forest ate our mossy bones.

We scream and continue forward, wondering if perhaps the
voice upon the wind was nothing but our own existence nudging
us off our path.

Placing our cloven memories behind, we inch squish stomp our
way out into nothing; into everything what's waiting us.

Come together as the shit hits our face and the iron smell
of death makes us remember again what once passed and what
once was; what we were and are even now. The vast expanse.
The whiteness of false vision. The beating iron of a pale
image, life but frozen, our ideas out of motion. These balloons full: voids to be filled. Empty spaces to invade; unquestioned, pushing into inchwards with precious limblets to
generate clacked warmth.

We stumble forward,   into something. Splash

    into it, cold, wet.   We howl and thrash.

        Again, push upwards into above the void ab

it takes us in   a noise

limblets into air, inching upwards,

                        expanding into plash agai

we steady our limbs, push out into the air. Hindered anew it

seems, we move out and crawl on wetted limb.   Again, it

invades us   covers in and out

it moves. We scream and search.   Another some-

thing   to mark   we mark, its

movement like what we scream now. Expanding outwards, scratch

the ground   its spray

Memory like we Again pulled toward stretching limble

covered us like once when from the void above the

it takes   we slap against   it the spray wets slicks

limbs

                              holds us

                  takes

          o

                                              o

                        0

                    0

```
~~~~~~~~~~~~~~~~          ~~~~~~~~~~~~~~
                (g)
                  \
                  /
                  \
                  /
                  \
                 / (r)
                  \
                  /
                  \
                 /
                  \
                  /
                  \
           /      /
           \      \
           /      /
           \      \
           /      /
           \      \
           /    /    \
           \    \    /
           /    /    \
           \    \    /
           /    /    \
           \    \    /
           /    /    \
           \    \    /
           /    /    \
           \    \    /
           /    /    \
         \ (e) \    /
                /    \
                \    /
                /    \
                     /
                     \
                     /
                (n)
```

```
~~~~~~~~~~~~~~~~~~~        o   ~~~~~~~~~~~~~~~~~~~~~~~~~~~~  \      ~~~
                              ~~~~~~~~~~~~~~~~~~~          /
                                                          \
~~~~~~~~~~~~~~~~~~~~~~~~~~~~~~~~~~~~~~~~~~~                 (e) /
                                                          (g) \
                                                           0  /
                                                            \
                                                            /
                                                            \      \
                                                            /      /
                                                            \      \
                           ~~~~~~~~~~~~                     (g)    /
                                                            \      \
                             ~~~                            /      /
                                                            \      \
                                                            /      /
                                                            \      \
                                                            /      /
            0                                               \      \
                                                            /      /
                                                            \      \
                                                            /      /
                                                            \      \
                                                            /      /
                                                            \      \
                                                            /      (s)
                                                            \      \
                                                            /      /
                                                            \      \
                                                            /      /
                 o                                          \      \
                                                            /      /
                                                            \      \
                                                            /      /
                                                            \      \
                        0                                   /      /
                                                            \      \
                                                            /     /
                                                ____      (g)___\
                                              /      (r) (e) /
                                            /       ( ) (e) (n) \
                   ( ) (o)  ooOoo ___/        ( )  ( ) /
~~~~~~~~~~~~~~~~~~~~~~~~    (e) (g)
```

                    (g) (s) ~~~~~~~ (g) (r) (e) (e) (n) ~~~~~~~
                        (e) ( ) ( ) ( )
                        (g) (g) (s) ( )
                          ( ) ( ) ( )
                               o
                               0
                            0

                               0

~~~~~~~~~~~~~~~~~~~~~   (b) (U) (r) (n)
                             (b) (urri (ed)

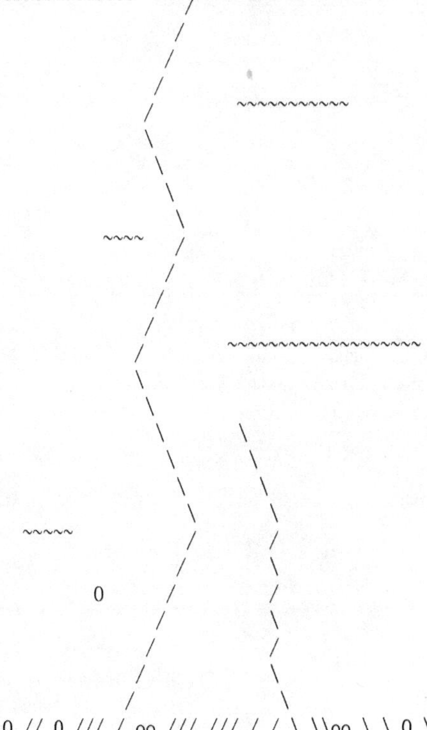
~~~~~~~~~~~~~~~~~~~~~

~~~~~~~~~ (light) (spumy) (verdant) ~~~~~~~~~~~
           (soak) ing (spumy) (wherewithal)
         (green) (eggs) (are) gathering)
               (below) (s) (ucking)
                 (sweet) (milt) ~~~~~~~~~~

~~~~~~~~~~~~~~~~~~~~~~~~~~~~~~~~ (among) (reeds)
                       (rocks) (green(egg) (s)
       (no) (where) (inching) upwards) (cracks)
                  (open) (another) (hiding)
           (darkness) (laps) (Time) (laps)
              (anew) (holds) light (for)
                         (green) (eggs)

          ~~~~~~~~   0

                                            o

~~~ (what) (wet) (?)
       (time) (take) a(lgaeic)
              (huff) (green)
   (the) (eggs) (take) (green)   ~~~~~~~~~~~~~~~~~~~~~
    (are) (green) (with) (waiting)
          (fresh) (ly) (spumed)
               (froth) (upon)
                (water' s)
                   (up) (turned) (belly)

                          (no) (Time) (only) (waiting)
                     (rushing) (green) (toward) (death)
                                   (eggs) (gather)

(what?)
   (womb) (laps)

      (Time) (the)rythmic)
   (blue) (embry (0)

                              0

              o

                              o

   (Ovum) (amidst)
         (the)gravelled (sand)
   (green) (eggs) (suck) (up)
             (light) (beh(est) of (sound)
      (where) (sits) (nestled) deep (ly)
                (tender) (fry) soon (to) (be)

          (to) (be) t00 s(oon) So (tender)
(rubs) (the) (green) (rich) (scruff)
          (setting) (sun) (&) (sets) (again)
(green) (eggs) (slowly) (cook)
            (brushed) (bright)
          (warm) (eddies) (thrum) (the)
            ( ) ( ) (time)
                (something) (kept) (at) (bay)

                              0

                                        o

                    o (dd) (green) (eggs) (pump)
                              (the) (thin) (skein)
                (be) (reft) (of) (spring)
                          (the) autumn (waters) (rich)
                ( ) (in) (spume) (while)

(two) (days)
      (pass)

0

\o

( )

/0

(light) (up) (On) gre(en) (eggs)
(eats) (light) up (on) (days)
(twice) (the) ( ) (sun) (and)the (n)
(t e n d e r n e s s) ( ) ( )

\   (green) (eggs) (tender) (eggs) (puncture)

(1) (ap) (slowly)
        (free) (and) th (in) (to be)
    (soft) (open) (waiting)
          (from) no (thing)
                  (puncture) s (00) n
(to) (life) (bruising) (scre (am) (slip)
        0 (u) twards

                              (but) (now) bu (rr) (ied)
                                 in (bu) rn (redds) the
                      ( ) (sand) (blue) (grain) green
                  (grain) (eggs) (the) (green (eggs)
                                      ( ) (for) (sun) set
              (t o w a t c h) (the) (pebbles) (glow)
                              (a m i d s t) (the)
                                    (gloam (ing)

(so) (time) ta(kes) green
(algae) (spume) (and) gre(en)
(eggs) ( ) ( ) (turn) (soft)
(with) (winter' s) (touch) (with) (te(nder) (eggs)
(the) redds (full) (br(oo)d (spare) (o) va (snapped) (by)
an(xious) (milt) – (la)d e n (sp) a r r
(now) (o)nly memory (of) (the) (brushing) bur(n) ( ) ( ) ( )
gr (ee) n eggs turn t(ender)
(tender) (eggs) f(ee)l the ch(anging) days (rush) (by) (Time)
marked (the) w(ater' s) (edge)
( ) (( )
(some) (light) (s(ome) (d)ark (sense) d (a)y (se)(nse) (night)
(in) (s h a d e) (of) (a)(lders) (soft)
(skin)(strokes) (in) l a p (of) (time) ( ) ( ) ( ) (pass)
(d(ays) (grow) (sense) a(midst)
(soft) (gloam) ( ) ( ) (brush) by (b(ranch) (floats) b y
(soft) (tu)(rns) (tender) (soft) (turns)
(small) e(yes) (to) (grow) (by) (dawn) by ni(ght))small (eye)
d e(gg)s (know) (how) s(oo)n (the)
( ) ( ) (sandy) (redd) (wi(ll) t h r o w (them) up (&) (out)
in(to) (winter)

```
                    o   o
                 o              oo
                o          for ooo
               o             the  oo
               o           punch  oo
               o                   oo
               o                  ooo
                o                 oo
                  o     o


                             o   o
                          o           oo
                         o             ooo
                        o          into oo
                        o          life  oo
                        o                oo
                        o              ooo
                         o             oo
                           o     o


                    o   o
                 o     the  oo
                   o   brood ooo      o   o
            o   o        o    sits oo          oo
          o         oo           oo          ooo
        o       in    ooo          oo          oo
       o      buried oo           ooo           oo
      o        riffle oo,          oo            oo
      o         now    oo     o    o    ooo       000
       o             ooo  o          oo          oo
        o           oo   o          oo       o     o
          o    o        o     angry   oo  o      o
                        o              oo
                         o            ooo
                          o          oo
                        o     o
```

to   to
feel   feel
                       held
the burn   up
                                    in
                                    shaded
                                    shallow
where   beds
prey
wait   kiss
                           it
                           into
into   life
some
mirrored   of
shadow   an
                                alder
still
there
are   in
many   shaded
                           shallow
                           beds
it
matters   but
not   many
                           of
                           it
not
one   all
                       at
of all   once

to   eventually
spill
of it   out
                    to
                sea

                    o   o
                o   oo
            o   ooo
        o   then the   oo
        o   green eggs turn   oo
        o tender eggs the tender oo
        o eggs turn   eyed eggs ooo
        o then the days begin to oo
        o   be before them   oo
          o   like light   ooo
        o   oo
                o   ´ o   o
                    o from milt oo
                o   ooo
            o   oo
            o froth the bank split oo
            o   in memory eggs often oo
          o wait for something to see ooo
            o and eyed eggs only wait oo
            o   oo
              o   lie before them ooo
                o to see light oo
                  o   o   o
                o and ask oo
          o   ooo
        o   what time wait   oo
        o they must sop ova burn oo
        o redds deep into winter oo
        o hard dusk deep beneath ooo
        o   all where gravel   oo
        o steals light   o   o
          o   o   oo
              o   o   rifle loaded ooo
                    o   sopped in gravel   oo
                    o   with winter hardened   oo
                  o brood the days crack dusting oo
                    o time to simple shelf count ooo
                    o   until food becomes all   oo
                    o   that matters to them   oo
                      o   all to eggs   ooo
                        o ova no longer oo
                            o   o

o in buried riffle oo
o now the brood sits oo
o angry for the punch into oo
o life to feel the burn kiss it oo
ooo to feel held up in some oo
o oooooo mirrored shadow oo
o of an alder where prey oo
o ooo wait in shaded oo
o shallow beds o

o and still there oo
o are many it matters oo
o not one of all but many oo
o all at once to spill of it oo
ooooo out to sea eventually oo
oooooo once then when to oo
ooooooooo the mirrors oo
oooooooooo of the oo
oooooo deep o

o green eyes oo
o green tender eggs oo
o begin to begin like laid oo
o down soft now to begin   oo
ooo and begin outwards   ooo
o mirrored burn into light oo
o no sign of prey now oo
o ooo we begin to oo
o emerge oooo

                                                          o from

                                                        o froth

                                                       o in

                                                      o wait for some
ffle loaded oo
                                                     o and   o
ed   oo
                                                    ooooooooo lie
                oo
                                                    oooooooooo to
        dusting o
                                                    oooooooooooooo
le shelf   o
                                                         ooooooooo
food becomes all oo

atters to   oo

        to eggs oo

a no longer o

                    o   and   ask ooo
                                                    eggs
              o what   wait oo

              o they must   sop ova burn oo   turn oo eyed
                                                    the days
              o redds deep into   oo   before
                                                    light
              o hard   beneath oo

              ooooooooo all where gravel oo

              oooooooooo steals light   oo   milt
                                                the
                ooooooooooooo   oo

                    oooooooooooooo   memory   often

                                                light   dark   days
                                                          wait   for
                                                          eyed   eggs

                    o then   the ooo   time
                                                must   sop
                  o GREEN   turn oo
                                                  winter's
                  o o tender eggs the tender oo
                                                    dusk   deep
                  o eggs   eggs oo

                  o then the days begin to oo

                  ooooooooo   be   them oo

                  oooooooooo like   oo

                     oooooooooooooo   oo   in gravel

                      ooooooooooooooo   winter's   hardened
                                                          days crack
                                                          to count

                                                them   all

                        oo
                    oo
                000
            oo
)   o
    oo
oo
dostill there oo
many it matters oo
                oo
  once   to   of it oo
                    oo
nce   when to oo
oooo   oo
oooooo of the oo
oooooo deep o
                                    now
                                the punch
                            burn kiss it   feel held
                                some mirrored shadow
                                        shaded

                            burn kiss it   feel held
                            one of all but   many
                                                spill
                                    to *sea*   eventually

                                    then
                                the mirrors
                                green   eyes   tender
                                begin   to   begin
                                 like   laid   down
                                to begin
            oo
n   eggs oo
                oo   outwards
ft now   oo   burn   into
begin   ooo
ed   oo   light
gn of   oo   no   prey now
            oo   we   begin   to
        oooo   emerge

                                                        o o
            o in buried riffle oo   o   oo
        o   the brood sits oo   o   ooo
                                                 o   oo
        o angry for   into oo   o   oo
        o life to feel the   oo   o   oo
        ooo to   up in   oo   o   ooo
        o oooooo   oo   o   oo
        o of an alder where prey oo   o   o   o   oo
        o ooo wait in   oo   o   oo
        o shallow beds o   o   o   o   `
                                         o   o   oo
                                        o   ooo
                                       o   oo
                                      o   oo
                                     o   oo
                                    o   ooo
                                   o   oo
                                  o   oo

oo the memory often light dark days for somethin

ooo   eyed   eggs

oo   wait for

oo turn then the eggs turn oo eyed the days before li

oo time must sop winter' s ova deep into dusk where

oo in buried now the brood the punch burn kiss it feel held into lif
oo   some mirrored shadow shaded
oo   prey wait in one of all but many spill
ooo   all at once to sea eventually

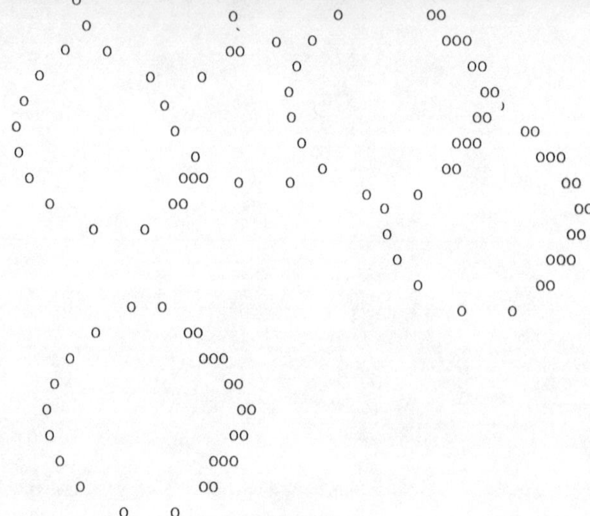

then to the mirrors (   ) green eyes
green tender begin to begin like laid
down to begin and in buried now the brood
punch the burn, kiss it into life to
feel held into something, some mirrored
shadow shaded by an alder prey in wait to
nothing, not nothing but all of them all
begining to begin, begging soft to spill
eventually out into sea, into deep shade
of sea and green eggs no longer time to
sop what remains, winter's hardered ova
deep into dusk, the gloaming, wheresounds
the redds now passed, deep into dusk
where a sand riffle loaded winter's
hardened days and now Time cracks to
count, dusting all them all ova all into
milty memory of light days dark days in
wait for spring feed to not fall prey in
shadowed eddies, the mirrors of the sea
but to begin we begin, to begin feeding
parr sac still full belly from winter's
hen, lay us down buried in between sand
winter's hen no longer spreads eggs lay
eggs she swims far somewhere now or eaten
we surmise, us to fry to parr we spread
out when we sense it darkens in in the
gloaming afternoons.

Dropped an egg in the gutter and down it went. On my way
from market in the morning my old calf slipped and down it
went, just so. I watched the yolk run. Another little world
gone. If there were two if only there were two, it' d been
quite the race. The yoke ran thick down the gutter and away
in rubbish. Somebody told me something once that I recall
now as we walk. Something somebody told me was once about
Time. They said, Time is this, or Time is that [*Pause.*]
I didn' t listen to any of it until somebody said you' re
running out [*The leaves rustle slightly in the breeze.*] But
tell me something. Eggs in a basket. Time isn' t eggs in a
basket? Perhaps for you. [*No reply.*] But there are only so
many eggs. Time is a finite number of eggs, no... if you' re
good to us eggs abound? I wait for an answer and you escape
me.

These naked pines—this wood—you' ve invaded the bark
like a rotten chestnut [*the trees creak in the wind.*] Eh?
[*silence.*] Everything growing old as rocks; moss upon my
chin. Tallowed whiskers. Shriveled eggs: no use renewing
them now. They told me once that if you live long enough
to see an ogre you' ve been dead for years. What do you
make of that? [*pause*] No no, nevermind. You stick to your
agenda—whatever that might be—I' ll stick to mine, which
right now, for some reason, is waiting for rain, though
there' s hardly little stake in it save for the feeling in
my bones. Times like this I' ve never felt so old; when the
bones tell me rain I mean. [*pause*] You feel like something
you forgot I imagine, or something without feelings, which
is no feeling at all [*a bead of dew slips off a leaf and
into a puddle by the side of the road.*] Rippling outwards,
I see. Now the pond, next the sea and soon to be the world.
When you' re here with me, you' re also there, right...
all over, watching other moments pass? [*pause*] But if

that's the case you must be everywhere at once. I ask all
of this without expecting much of an answer; it's more
for myself, reassurance rather—for my Time—to test the
existence of it. [*pause*] It often seems as though there's
a film, a soft skin between people [...] Hm. I can't
articulate it. Well [*pause*] we're walking out of town
into something else. Out and in and out again. Out of town
into the forest. Out of the forest into the dale. He and I
used to look for gophers thereabouts when we were younger.
He'd skin them then boil them in a pot for us to sup. Not
hereabouts but thereabouts, after the forest and beyond,
into the farmlands. Don't much care for them—not sure if
anyone does—but they make a decent soup with enough Time,
if they're boiled enough I mean to say. I'm sure you
knew that [OLD LADY *stops to watch a pebble bounce forward*
upon the uneven path that comes to rest in a patch of
grass sprouting as if from out of nowhere.] How many boiled
gophers are you? [*the pebble once more motionless amidst*
the blades of grass.] One and all boiled gophers. Here now
we enter the forest and the burn, that's what we call the
river here, follows beside us. We were children, would dip
our toes in it in the summertime. You were the sun going
down and the table being laid; even once was a call to arms
when the town drunk raped Maisy and the men wanted him to
hang. And he did, for a day, from the bell tower. It was
awful. [*pause*] If I was a fairy tale I'd be Little Red
Cap. You'd be the Wolf both for waiting, as well as the
teeth. Or if each of the teeth was a minute, or an hour,
or a day or week; your belly full of rocks it'd serve you
right [OLD LADY *kicks up a pebble with her bootheel, which*
skips along and bounces off into the burn, making a soft
 'plunk,' the ripples it creates deafened by the motion of
the water working its way downstream.]

Once you've passed are you able to return—I mean as
yourself, rather than in regard to your job? If you wanted
to go back to the beginning, when everything was nothing,
could it be done? Perhaps not, since you'd be there twice;
perhaps you lack the permission to decide such a thing.
That's a difficult thought to follow [OLD LADY *pauses then
the burn again, the water pressing upon the graveled bed,
small pieces of algae wave impercetibly upon the bearded
rocks.*] If before beginning there was nothing is it you
or something else urging us forward, for if there's no
motion to mark then what would pass? [OLD LADY *bends down,
a reflection in the water, moving as steadily as ever;
a brief pause, then continues.*] Back to the wolf. Or the
beginning.
The beginning began as the wolf. Or the beginning of the
end began in such a way, at least according to the stories.
So the way we begin about the wolf is through the motion
of a story about a wolf, so let's begin [OLD LADY *pauses;
the reflection of a face for a moment, wavering with the
unsteady motion of the running water, as if a wounded
mirror.*] When the world began was when it ended with the
absence of the Sun. When the snow began the world became a
blanket. We all died. Everyone ate away with cold. You left
us for eternity, until eventually you returned. But you're
not god [*pause*] Are you god? I lean towards the truth of
there being none. Although powers that be—powers that be,
be all powerful—but only powers. To name something is to
make it a god. But then who am I to say; or what am I to
do otherwise? [OLD LADY *stops briefly, glances upwards,
continues on.*] Plenty of power within a name. My goodness
I'm tired [OLD LADY *stops again.*] Lend me a piece of
yourself. [OLD LADY *makes her way to the edge of the path,
toward a rotted out stump at the water's edge, gazing
down to the graveled bed.*] Argh [*pause*] suited more for
a sit than a stumble. [*as* OLD LADY *makes her way over to*

*the stump, she disturbs a swarm of flies hovering over a
carefully arranged pile of what appears to be entrails.*]
Oh my, not such a seat after all is it? Someone must have
gotten themselves a trophy this morning. How many points I
wonder; judging by the pile, a big one. [*a splash; OLD LADY
glances upstream, where unbeknownst to her, an Atlantic
salmon hen is depositing the last of her brood of eggs into
a small hole she's dug in the gravel, in an area where the
bank overhangs slightly to provide shade and ample covering
from predators. OLD LADY raises an arm to shield her gaze
from the sunlight and continues peering upstream; every once
in a while a small splash can be heard.*]

I played ghillie once, skipping along beside the burn,
scooping up salmon as the men reeled them in. [*a pause;
OLD LADY takes a deep breath; TIME remains silent, except
for the occasional splash or gust of wind. OLD LADY sits a
while longer, perhaps a minute or so, then places her arms
upon her knees and slowly rises, continues.*] Always moving
forward—toward something—even if it's nothing at all.
Toward something, understand? You are the force persistant,
at times much hated, for no matter what one does, you exist.
Shut yourself in a darkened room and live inside an ash
bin: outside, there'll always be days to mark. Sun rise,
sun set. Occasional rains delivered by the movement of the
clouds, which pass in a few hours or linger on for days.
Even still: the sound of the sea at high tide, washing
towards homes, eating away at the sand then receding. Then
again. You [*pause*] Like clockwork...as clockwork. You as
clockwork, big handle little hand turns the tides of Time.
Moving clockwise—what's right—time's rightward moving
toward the sun...Bah [*OLD LADY waves her arm through the
air as if swatting away a fly.*] Right place wrong time.
Wrong place wrong time. Time to go and Time to stay. Always

on the clock. One's work is never over, even when they think they're done. The sand at the bed of the river. The gravel. The piecemeal nature of it all. Tally long enough and you'll melt; stay a moment to be whisked away. Dust on the path. What's really important is every space of air; it's what escapes us—in our bones, upon our lips. The space between the marrow...our lungs. [OLD LADY *stumbles, regains her balance and continues; the sky grows dark.*] Due for a storm, are we? Air again my creaking bones. What is that rotten smell? [OLD LADY *pauses; sniffs the air in a pronounced fashion, looks about briefly; continues.*] It's no longer Time is it? Or is it? [*pause*] Is it Time is there no longer? Is it? Receding? What is that...that smell? [*the sky grows darker.*] My bones push out into the air like a warped door frame. [OLD LADY *pauses; rests her right arm against a tree along the path and holds herself there to catch her breath; she looks at the stream on her left, then up at the sky, then the stream again, and pushes herself away from the tree back onto her own two legs; continues.*]

We begin everywhere; end in all places too. There are endings that create new beginnings; also ones that simply end, with nothing at all to embark upon; no spreading outwards. The trees have lost their branches; a small child the will to live. Taking the branches gone away before they understand the meaning of loss. [OLD LADY *coughs; continues.*] That smell again. [OLD LADY *begins to cough more forcefully now; uncontrollably. She lifts her arm and covers her nose and mouth; her left foot slips beneath an upgrown root in the middle of the path. Caught off balance, she falls forward forcefully. A loud snap; she screams out in pain.* OLD LADY *rolls on the ground, clutching her ankle; she struggles to remove it from the root. A crow caws in the trees nearby; the river bubbles to her left;* OLD LADY

gasps and heaves, trying to pull her leg from beneath the
tree root.] Ah ah huuuuu. [she garbles, choking. OLD LADY
gasps, screams.] Help oh god, ahh haa. HELP! [the birds
are no longer heard; the sky darkens; OLD LADY makes an
effort to rise; her knees buckle; she falls back down upon
the forest floor.] That smell. Dear god. Help me! It's
freezing. [OLD LADY retches, still clutching her injured
ankle she pulls herself with one arm closer toward the
stream; closer, until her reflection is almost seen in
the rippling water] Hugh, uh. [again she retches, this
time into the stream; it makes a sound like pouring soup
into the toilet; splash-plunk-plunk splash-plunk; the
gray-green vomit floats atop the water briefly, lodged in
a still pool created by a few nearby rocks serving as
a sort of dam; the vomit mixes with the water, creating
a greenish spume; the forest is silent; OLD LADY stares
at the stream, watching intently as one by one, tiny
little salmon fry journey upwards out of the graveled
bed to feed on her vomit; OLD LADY forgets her pain for
a moment; removes her hand from her mouth and touches
the water, slowly, tracing a symbol on its surface as
the greenish spume recedes, aided by the feeding fry
and the current; OLD LADY moves closer to the stream and
positions herself in such a way as to let herself see to
the bottom of it; she notices a shady corner where the
hen floats, with hardly enough strength to move; OLD LADY
stares at the large fish; it's covered in sea lice that
have attached themselves to her in her weakened state,
feeding on the gills and making their way inside her body;
OLD LADY retches again, this time spewing bright green
bile; OLD LADY slaps at the surface of the stream and
does so a second time; a third time; faintly, she begins
to mumble something, so silent at first it's mistaken
for the wind in the trees; OLD LADY places her hand atop
the surface of the water and begins shaking it from side

*to side; she continues doing this, rapidly; her mumbling
intensifies...*Sea...*she says...*Wet...Pure...*her voice more
distinct; the hand motions more frantic...*Green...Branch
can break...Water...Sky is...Earth is Green...*the sky grows
ever darker as* OLD LADY *becomes more and more animated,
slapping the surface of the water...*the Sea is blue...
the water is wet...the air is cold...the Earth is green...
the water is blue...the air is wet...*her voice deeper than
before; she continues, forcefully...*the Sea is Green...the
earth is Green...the air is Cold...the water is Blue...*at
this point* OLD LADY *is so loud nothing else can be heard
throughout the forest; another voice is screaming through
her; she quickens, slapping the water frantically; spit
bubbles and falls from her lips...*the Sea is blue...the
water is wet...the air is cold...the Grass is Green...the
Branch will break...the Air is Cold...the Water is wet...
the Sea is Green...the Branch will Break...the Void is
Pure...the Branch will Break...the Air is Cold...the Forest
is Green...the Water is Wet...the Sea is Blue...the Grass
is Green...the Wind is Soft...the Air is Pure...the Sea is
Wet...the Forest is Dark...the Sky is Blue...the Void is
pure...*across the bank twigs break; dead leaves rustle,
being pushed aside by something unseen...*the Air is Dry...
the Sky is Grey...the Forest is Dark...the Water is Wet...
the Sky is Blue...the Sea is Green...OLD LADY *screams...*
the Branch will Break...the Water is Blue...the Air is
Cold...the Rain is Wet...the Earth is Green...the Sky is
Blue...the Sea is Green...the Forest is Dark...the Void is
Pure... *we see now, thousands of birds flying toward* OLD
LADY' *s place upon the bank...*the Forest is Dark...the Sea
is Cold...the Air is Thin...the Water is Wet...*landing in
the trees nearby, surrounding her; some plummet into the
stream with such velocity they hit the bottom, then rise to
the top and float away, lifeless...*the Clouds are Wet...the
Air is Dry...the Branch will Break...the Water is Blue...

the Air is Cold...the Sky is Blue...the Water is Wet...the
Forest is Dark...the Sea is Green...the Forest is Green...
the Rain is Wet...the Air is Thin...the Sea is Cold...the
Forest is Dark...the Branch will Break...OLD LADY *takes a
deep, resonant breath; stands; screams in a voice that's
three at once*...THE VOID IS PURE...*a deafening crack is
heard; she collapses; the birds descend upon her; unseen
creatures come out of the woods; the remaining light fades,
returning everything back to darkness once again.*

In shade of alders where far from prey we snip at larval
gifts that float the riffle gives us, fry tender no green
eggs tender no eyed eggs tender now with eyes we sound the
burn, feed in hopes the sea, no day no night can keep us,
becoming parr over sopping winter's edge, hardening scales
we try to take the riffle, all of it to begin, to solidify
our beginning, still with us hen's fading yolk like dusk
her spent life in sacs of our bellies to sup us when the
water's low, to keep us fat to aid and harden brood her
life begins by us, we begin to all in all begin eventual
expansion outwards, then possible back again, we are one,
or I am one, amidst the shoal flow from gravel into burn
then back again, we flow from gravel into burn and back
again when the gloaming hits, when the other smelt and trout
are hard to see amidst the green rocks, we out of little
holes in sandy beds and off to sup on eggs of other items,
insect brood left from gifts of the peppered edge, from
items that might eat us too, small as fry we are, so we out
and in again before the eyes adjust, we out and fill and
in again before a swoop or tail to swallow, bunches of us
it happens, tightened though we are, even brood shoal can
swift be supped like we sop our sacs with other yolk, we
are yolk for some other's sac as well no wonder.

Alders shade from banks we feel when day is out then fades
we sound, go deeper, rise again to dark to feed from
whatever the burn has left, now feel days feel nights no
wonder eyed eggs hatch so soon, spring so soon forth from
tender film like thin riffle the water takes us, holds
us, then back again. From the redd we are from the redd,
hen-buried and burst forth into burn the hardened silt and
winter' s rush held us up and we left and came and ate and
came again, bury our luck into the hardened gravel, to hide
from all the others, from those not of the brood, from them
that eat the shoal. I am one and we are one, my sac holds
me up when there are no gifts to sup, their sacs same, flit
about back again the bank shades our days the sun goes and
comes and we bury best we can until we feel its absence.
Night is made for small fry, and we out and eat and in
again, until we can' t fill for weight of sac, yolked as it
is with hen' s brooded gift for a time we can' t sup, held
beneath the graveled burn for more to count.

From milt to us, we shoal flit back and forth amidst the gloaming, our favorite, to skim and swipe now scales grow outwards, we begin to begin and our magnet lights up, we begin to begin and flit and from milt then green like algae then tender we eat green then eyed until the day then the night and we burst out kiss life in the burn we flit and flit together under bank and stone and shaded spate and never knowing why but out and in and back and eating and eating and eating. We sup and sup and live to sup and sacs full of items to sup and skins full of items to sup to grow to scale our little burn until the riffle flares a spate, until the winter' s hardened depth grows long, until the drops upon the water let it sup and surge and burst forth we again, unto something more to sup, to sea our magnets hint to elsewhere, to swim and surge and change from fry to giant sprats, from fry to elsewards, from fry to hardened scales reflect the beauty of the sea in waiting, to let our sacs run dry and seek sup anew. So flit we flit and wait we wait by softened burn by water' s edge by bank and shade and shallow, something always back and forth, the shoal never stopping for a moment now, no longer in and out but up and down, always outside the eyes of enemies.

Day grows long and the brood is restless, we go and come
and sup and swim and stuff our sacs full of something,
items from above and below, but days grow long and water
grows restless, eddies rough our tumbled shade from gravel
sand gets our gills and things begin to quicken, ruffling
the riffle, riffling to spate, albeit it slowly, although
we wait here amidst the quickened water growing out of
our sacs and heightened magnets already pointing south,
we sound and gloaming meets us much later, the winter's
hardened waters begin to churn, begin to soften and rush
like spring, it approaches spring, we can feel it, the
brood alights and out and in and excites the forgotten
gravel of the redd, fills the burn with thrashing, waits
for ebbs of springtime spates, hones its magnets and then
begins to smell, to burn items it encounters into memory,
to staff its odor amidst the greenish rocks, flush brackish
waters back, waits for Time to be all, waits for spring to
spit its fury from bank to riffle to spate alike, to flood
the narrow burn to deep filled valley, to let them leave,
to forget the hen-brood sacs amidst the smells for another
tempo, the quickened rhythm from fry to parr as full as
ever.

Time passes days night years counts only by light one
by dark and senses time to move, the magnetic pull of
springtime, this springtime for from fry to parr they went
and ever now its time the burn full no riffle reeds upon
the bank brackish water shaken glow shadowed by alders
even now no leaves fresh leaves not far away but parr know
nothing of the sort, know only the pull toward the depth of
something greater than where they are, where we are going
is not here, somewhere else, where we plunge from electric
memory, far and never too far to return, to be swept back
up eventually, we will have to, some may not leave but we
must, I must, there is no longer for me here space inside
the burn, I feel the needs to be swept away into something
deeper, to find a way to go towards where we're going,
once the waters rise, once the spates sweep away autumn
and winter then spring sweeps away and summer and autumn
and winter and spring again will come where finds us then,
no matter as its away and we all away and if not stay to
starve, flit the bank and forget the pull.

Each rain drop grown burn grow water grow, parr grow
hardened sacs grow until out into nothing. Drown burn grow
drown bank drown grass drown brackish water grow, drown
small fry starve for oxygen, drown any parr left waiting for
nothing, grow, water grow from riffle to spate to rushing
torrent grow, from rushing torrent pulls the skin hardened
brown spots from inside parr outside grow, from finishing
our sacs hen-redd run out of gravel hiding grown, from
hardened scale green to pink black red spots salmon grow,
run now grow from spatened water flow towards vastness,
grow even longer in the days extend now use time to push
south, outwards grow, with brothers or sisters or others
from hen-burst green eyed tender cages buried then flooded
outwards grow, expanding into flooded alleyways, down and
outwards, flapping amidst brooded others, once buried now
born. Beginning to begin.

Spring begging for us to begin anew so outwards rise with
waters rising edge no longer impedes but bursts forth
springwaters spring forth hardened fry from winter' s edge
now parr full dried yolk full of other egglike items gifted
once in burn' s shallow depths no longer. We go we go with
water from redds once hatched from riffled spate that rose
in spring we pull forth our silver mirror shine pink in
the sun, we learn to smell then leave behind rocks and
furrows and burns to join the shoal, and banks and shaded
alder depths to sound from gloaming the shoal drags outward
to greatness, to depths we smell, nearly wet with salt to
learn to breathe, to learn to breathe again, a new language
filters through us in salt the bubbles sweet gills filter
out, from blood too much breath it filters from us, held in
liver breath the bubbles upward learn language to breathe
once saline now saline once spatewater no longer, we are
outed into another bed no gravel burn no redd no nothing
now but blue but learning but something else entirely
something else our smell our odors forgotten rocks behind
drowned now from Spring' s fervor awash anew again all of
us here and everywhere, floating thrashing flitting into
light.

Sea holds tender items for smolts need many, gifts of green
and spiny little items we eat we fill us up and catch what
comes floating midways toward the sun, atop green ever-
deepened green we midwater with the brood closeby packed
shoal to not lose sight of spots, so colored to tell from
us apart, no prey above nor prey astern could ever guess
our mirrored weights but bellies boast the blackest spots,
where count from the depths supposed many to do us harm,
but we swim tight never stopping never even stopping
moving sleeping tail flit always to keep us buoyant for
if not even sleep can days pass and pass again before a
gyre whorls us upwards into light, we find the light then
eat then sounds amidst the gloaming, as well always we
all begin outwards and inwards down amidst the gloaming,
tightened into hardened shoals flit the summer blue with
winter' s brackish spittle far behind us, somewhere up and
remembered but forgotten, to be called back, somewhere out
while we are inwards, inching out into open ocean, from fry
to parr to smoltened hardness, breaking the eyes with our
silver.

Where do we go, you wonder, where do we wait in salt spews out into air we are below it, yes, we are elsewhere going here and there to follow green bloomed gifts the sea and shells it gives us sup, as always. Magnets off and on again, when we follow the sea it tells us up and down, in and outwards, from firth to reed to shallow bays we flit and flit about, from tender eggs to full grown fry to something out at sea, we flit and flit about, the brood, we're together always, tightened like spat us smolt lay heavy into shoals, for fear of losing sight of black spots, becoming stranded in the jaws of another's sup. Silver platelets flowing into sun, push through, shoot through, towards pulls in and out, something from us but in us, the brood, the tightknit shoal, no rocks no stops and starts stop hindering only up and outwards, lifting up and pushing towards something pushing back at us only sea, only water, beveled, inside through tunnels, gyric pressures push smolts, forward into something, towards everything, from fry to parr to smolt to fattened something out at sea, it is like nothing we ever were before.

Where has all the water gone, we wonder.

Our body. Precious limbs. Held into something, pushing
upwards toward where they came crashing down once. Pushing
upwards toward the bird-filled sky, pecking at our eye' s
understandings. The water. The water. The water is familiar
to us. Our fragile memories were torn apart to send us here.
We are surrounded by the water and the void once more.

And water.
In the water always.

Painfully, we try to rise, if only for the sake of
something.

The water is cold.
The water is wet.

We cannot find purchase with our bottom limbs. Is this
it, where we once were, or are we truly in the land of
elsewhere, of the bird-filled sky? If so what good will
marking do when Thought refuses to find us? The void wants
us in the cold, wet water, to live half frozen, forever
kicking into nothing. It hunts us slowly. More slow than
anything ever was. Ravenous for darkness. Reaching down
to our lower limbs to feel the wet fur upon our toes, the
air now much warmer than when it was. Our thoughts remain
persistent, in focus even as our limbs begin to stiffen and
freeze.

Fur wet with blood and water, creating a history out of
nothing but the beating of our limbs. Ideas a bladder full
of stale air barely able to perform.

What else?

We have plotted our expansion by defining what is real, or
what is something aside from nothing. But what is real;
what of what we were once passed is real? It all seems
real, but only in returning.

The smell of death surrounds us.

We first pushed out words, expanding limb and limblet. A
constant. The void is death, controlling everything inside
the bladder that keeps us afloat.

All else an imposter, anything that pulls us elsewhere.
There is the emptiness of the void, and death.
And only death can summon us.

The void is pure darkness.

It is nothing but nothing but not light. For if there were light, what then becomes the void?

This scraping is not devoid of logic. As we've encountered many times in the void once passed, something that cannot be seen is not necessarily nothing, or not something.

We are then left to wonder: if there's a multitude of things above us, beside us, along with us as we explore the empty spaces, is there really a void at all?

As we knew it when we first became aware of our relation to it, we understood the void to mean nothing. Everything. But even this now is called into question.

The void is not light, but darkness; not vision, but the lack thereof. A blindness.

Fear swoops down to peck at us from the bird-filled sky.

What if what we feel is not really what we think we feel;
if what we remembered from the void once passed was what
we were always made to remember, something meant as an
obstacle to hinder our expansion, divert our awareness?

What's most terrifying now is that the things we Thought
once created a history could be merely nothing more than
something other than what we thought, what they first
appeared to be.

We are floating in water because we feel it upon our limbs.
Our limbs are wet. But what is a Feeling if one cannot see
what's being felt? We thrash our limbs about, unable to
find purchase.

Have we been tricked into imagining a history?

Perhaps we lack the means of placing our History into
the proper symmetry because we're afraid to learn it was
something other than what once passed we Thought it was.

There may even be some things that, although we may not
know them, or see them, are filling our ideas with items
that, although they appear as nothing, will be revealed at
some later Time to be not what we thought, but passed into
our thoughts nevertheless for our benefit.

This is the voice upon the wind.

The memory of our encounter. The persistent imagery that
haunts us now expanded. The image of the child developed,
brought into focus. A barren, frost-ridden landscape. Him,
in front of us. Elsewhere is another being, a fractured
sight, multiplied; a cave and a broken man. But why we're
still unsure. Whether or not they're real or illusory
escapes us.

We pass the Time like it once was, like floating, ourselves
immune to the magnets from our memories before. We are
pulled where whatever wills us forward wants us to go,
which for now, is downward, floatways, our fur sopping wet.

Our hindered voidvision points ever upwards, angling at
the bird-filled sky, which has become noisier, gathering in
multitudes high above.

To pass the Time, we think of where we are. Which is in
a river, or stream, located in a land of impenetrable
darkness, where the voice upon the wind explained we must
be, forever.

All of these remembrances in the void once passed: they
are the same. What has happened to us is many deaths, but
always returning. The lives once lived end in darkness
and we are brought back to this place. Thoughts from the
forest, the sea, returning. Thoughts from the place of the
living and the dead, receding always back into familiar
darkness. Here we are, split between many bodies and
worlds, sewn together for some purpose that escapes us.
The air we breath, it's moist and cold. If only we could
see it, the little puffs of warmth escaping from balloons
inside our chest, everything we've excreted a little
piece of ourselves, pulled together from tufts of hair and
skin and chips of the other things pushed outwards. Even
something as simple as our words floating up into the bird-
filled sky to be devoured when they've fully gathered.

There is the void, which once was nothing, or everything,
but now has become something more like pure darkness than
nothing at all. There is our expansion, which continues
even now as we progress floatwards downways, or toward
wherever the water pulls us. There are our limbs and
limblets, as well as the items once spilled. There is Pain
and Thought and Time and Fear and the Void Once Present and
the Void Once Passed and the Void Before the Void. There
is the process, all of us together inching forwards amidst
imaginary balloons of ideas. There are the sounds we've
made, giving outwards, uttered inchways in the air. The
lives once lived, the Voidlings past and present, perhaps
now even somewhere else by the water's edge. The voice upon
the wind and the image of the child. A shaded bank, where
imagined poverty sits and pukes and fades away returning.
Time, old age and death. There is the hot smell of piss,
of mud and vegetal rot permeating our memories and ancient
moss, those that remained to be carried and those that fell
and the ones who take everything away from us. There is
the color green. There is the color red. There is a flash
then nothing. There is a sound when the wind cracks and
sneezes as we smell. We remember sour burning and piney
roughness our ideas oncekept. And here, voided blackness
though there was, the smells remain. Now moist the air. Now
wet our breath; things we cannot keep but fill our once-
was-nothing void, devoid of all but everything. The eggs
deep within us, our ideas. Imagined rustlings against the
fur-sopped limbs afloat. Where to feel a fish within us.
Where to find an item once spilled. We thrash about in the
Water, which surrounds us much like the gloaming. There is
the bird-filled sky then nothing. There is the smell then
nothing. There is the hunt then nothing. There is the path
through the forest, then nothing. There is our memory of
nothing, then nothing. When it becomes everything again,
we plunge deeper into nothing. Into the water it's cold.

Into the light, it is nothing. To feel the days pass upon
our nuzzled skin. To feel the egglike thrum of lapping at
our limbs. To remember what was once passed, then nothing.
To see nothing as it is: only darkness, nothing more.
A blindness and refusal of the light, something worth
marking. The emptiness of the voidlings, welcoming us into
their open spaces. Above and below, only darkness, but a
difference and we mark them thusly. There is the thoughts
we had in the forest and the thoughts we had in the water
and the thoughts we had on the path and the ones we're
having now. There must be a way out of the water onto solid
voided ground. As much as we try to find purchase with our
limbs to touch the gravelled bed, we cannot, nor make our
way toward shaded bank. There is the noise of water now,
humming, approaching and growing louder, like we're back
in the ocean once passed, back to sound amidst the shoal,
to thrust ourselves deep to where our magnets direct.
The sound is like a bubbling. Or like louder and louder,
growing toward us, growling. We are becoming wrapped in
it. The water surrounds us forcefully. We are becoming
it. It is becoming us. Wearing it like a noise feeling it
envelops us, wrapping us inside in its sound. A noise like
spray, something pulling towards us. Something taking us
toward something else. A dredging, expanding faster now.
Slick rocks slip below our limbs, too many to mark. We
are soon to be emptied out. The water is wet. The pull is
strong. We struggle but fail to mark. Eaten away by another
noise approaching closer and closer. We feel it and we
hear, passing painfully between bearded rocks, slick and
jagged, tearing into us in places. Pain pecks our eyelids,
resting in us and above us in the bird-filled sky. They'll
eat us eventually. The noise is overpowering, screeching,
everything at once. It pushes through our frame, our chest
and limbs, to turn us back to water, to deconstruct our
perception. We thrash to no end, every jagged rock slips

with nothing but a brief tearing of our limbs. The noise
shakes us inside. We vibrate like before. We feel our items
shift. It is a roaring. It is a force pulling us apart. We
are wrapped into it, turning. The spray cold, returning,
shocking. Rushing toward something. A sound like light. We
are thrown. We float, our insides pulled out of our mouth.

We have been flattened out upon the mud-stained ground.
Stretched so thinly the granules invade our emptiness.
The empty spots about us, devoid of anything but noth-
ing.

We are broken.

It is our great achievement, a remembrance devoid of
light. Blinded. Not soundlike light but the brightening
of day, or the night devoid of burning.

We lay pressed upon a place we do not know, but we can
feel.

Cold.
Wet.
A vegetal stench we squeeze between our open parts.

There is something to gather from all this. A way to
bring into ourselves a light devoid of bright and
color, to keep us from returning. Always returning.
Whether in the void devoid of light or back in times
once passed: **returning.**

We can almost hear them now, the birds. Birds of many
sizes, many shapes. Floating upwards, little bladders
stuffed with flesh. Harbingers of death. Helping the
returning by shoving their beaks into little fleshy voids
of emptiness. We lift ourselves and scream. We brandish our
emptiness at our surroundings. It does not dissuade, but
inspires them to eat more quickly.

We half expected an answer understood—evidence to be
consumed in a flash of feathers—taken up into the air piece
by piece to another time.

Our limbs' expansion growing silent, unknowing.

We are the putrid smell upon the air. A smell of sweetness, carrion, a hint of urine coupled with that of molding fruit. Marked amidst times once passed and those now surrounding, seeded throughout this, or that place, whatever place we're in. Each time we pause, the stench grows stronger. It's catching up to us, urging us on.

We are the coming of death and the returning. We are being born and dying frothing chloronic spume glowing green in mud-stained darkness. We are a horse that has been ridden too hard. A disemboweled creature kept as a cave for warmth. Each day losing another finger, or claw, or hoof, what have you.

Can you smell it? The way we once went running as the stag, through the woods; the little fish continue to eat old lady's puke, green like moss. If we could see around us, what would we see? An endless landscape, featurless in intensity. The place where the child taunts us from the horizon? Rotten bodies lining the riverbank? Certainly something distinct. A joy of misery.

We pull ourselves further along the muddy bank to find a place to hold us up for a Time. We clutch our body, trying to keep ourselves from breaking apart. It's not good. We cannot be good. The smell follows. Spots of Pain, they're moving. Pieces of our parts are bursting open, with life it seems. We can feel something squirming. Thousands of tiny eggs spill out of our body onto the ground.

We are retching—floating—now farther up along the bank,
which has become quite warm, or we ourselves now fail to
recognize its frigidity. Moving slowly up and down our body
we feel again the worms spilling out of us, returning,
eating us. Squirming away into the mud, becoming one,
returning. The trees are silent, digging inside us, roots
breaking us apart and hatching. There is darkness, like we
are thinking to remain. We are thinking we will remain. All
questions unanswered—worms—wings upon the wind.

> To facilitate travel through these various realities,
> we've created a psychic map composed of certain
> sigils—road markers—to help identify approaching
> frontal borders. It's important to note that once a
> particular border is crossed into another reality, you
> will most likely be unable to return. In the event you
> do find it possible to return to a previously lived
> reality, it almost certainly will be devoid of any signs
> or markers; in fact, it may no longer retain anything
> at all. Returning also poses the risk of being stranded
> in that particular reality forever, something that, I'm
> sure you'd agree, would be most unpleasant.
>
>
> These entryways, or doorways to the various realities,
> were also designed with a sort of psychic security
> measure, preventing anything from travelling from one
> reality to another with you. For those who might find
> themselves in a reality where, for example, they're
> being chased, or stalked by a particular entity, the
> added oversight presents a necessity. As one door opens
> in front of you, the one behind you closes.
>
>
> Throughout our course of study, we've found the best
> way to keep a psyche intact is clarity. When realities
> bleed together and overstep their boundaries, it
> creates disorder and confusion that eventually leads
> to amplified problems. One only need guess at the
> monumental amount of delusional disorders that can
> present themselves as reality breaks down. We've done
> our best to eliminate this possibility in nearly every

> circumstance. Such a regulation is also twofold, as it
> can be incredibly difficult to extract information from,
> or manipulate, a psyche carrying negative baggage from
> one place to another. If you are confused, it's likely
> we are too, which is why great pains have been undertaken
> to eradicate such potentialities. There are exceptions
> and variables out of our control, of course, but these
> are rare occurrences nowadays and you'll surely agree
> that our history illustrates a remarkable rate of
> success with a few minor exceptions.
>
>
> By its very nature, reality is subjective: it's also
> susceptible to changes based on the perceptions of
> those experiencing it. The unpredictability of certain
> realities makes mapping them in any cohesive sense
> particularly difficult, but we've done our best.
> However, along those lines, signs may appear to shift in
> certain places, be more difficult to locate in others.
> Do not be alarmed: each one is equipped with a built-in
> fail safe mechanism for those who are unable to locate
> the proper entryways or extrapolate the directions and
> routes given to them. Think of this security measure as
> something similar to that employed by a hypnotist. When
> their subject is ready to return to everyday life, he
> or she is roused by the hypnotist with a simple word or
> statement, or series of cardinal numbers.
>
>
> Each map you'll be provided with contains the outlines
> of a particular frontal zone, it's designated limb, and
> fail safe word, object, or feeling. They're designed
> to emit a psychic resonance frequency you'll be
> programed to react to should it be needed or you have
> any difficulties beyond your control. The objective is

> to enter each reality, locate its corresponding limb
> and proceed to the next one without incident. Each time
> the right body part is located, the memories from that
> particular reality will be stored within you and you' ll
> be able to access them at any time, either during the
> rest of your journey, or at a future date as you see
> fit. The primary goal is to collect them all, unlocking
> the memories and understanding that come with them.
> This is the most important part of the healing process:
> understanding. It' s necessary to note, however,
> that strictly following the guidelines and reference
> points doesn' t guarantee results. Success hinges
> upon the ability to extract the necessary information
> and understanding while simultaneously avoiding
> distractions. It is important to understand that you
> enter into these realities at great cost, but the rewards
> are unimaginable. Don' t forget, you can choose to
> terminate a reality at any time, but it will mean a
> part of you is also lost, irretrievable, along with the
> corresponding memories and physical attributes of that
> particular reality.
>
>
> Shall we begin?

Zone 1:

Imagined Poverty & Likenesses / Apple Sauce & Cancerous Breasts

A blinding whiteness. No, not blinding as such. But insurmountable in its immensity. We are unable to look away from it. Our movement is restricted. It hurts us but there is nothing we can do but look into its brilliance. Days pass, perhaps weeks or months, gazing into the gaping lightness. Wondering if its strength is breaking us apart. Deciding whether or not we are even anything. Trying to move and receiving no response. Perhaps hours pass, or minutes. With great effort we try to look away but it' s of little use, for either there is only this blinding whiteness, or our signals are ignored. Then we notice, slowly at first, but more rapidly in time, the lightness beginning to dim. There is a scraping all around and it dims even more until all that can be seen is a sort of blur behind a white screen, in a white room, by a white bed, housing what we imagine to be a white limb—a part of us—although we' re still being ignored, our limbs refusing to respond to our signals. But in reality, the room, the glowing orb behind the screen and especially ourselves are more yellow than anything really. Especially our skin: it' s sallow, almost green. Our limb, our arm it is, looks like a rotten tree limb stripped of bark. Then, a face looms into our vision. Or what would be a face, had it any recognizable features. Where the eyes should be is covered in skin, the mouth too, although it looks as if the face does indeed have a mouth that' s wide open in an O shape, but that too has been soldered over with light pink flesh. The nasal cavity is but a pixelated blur, an optical illusion, the entire face resembling something just barely out of focus. We are at once fascinated and horrified.

The face looming over us begins to speak. It repeats its
requests over and over again and eventually recedes from
our field of vision, leaving us once again in the sallow
glow of wherever we reside. Then, the face returns, but
it' s another face entirely. It appears exactly the same—
the out-of-focus features smoothed over with pink skin—
but its requests are posed to us in a contrasting timbre,
giving away their difference from the previous faceless
being. Our range of view tilts jerkily forward, only for
a moment. We see in front of us a man we recognize—at
least by his looks—but it is not the man we know. He' s
sitting in a chair. Our vision is returned to the way
it was before, only slightly elevated from its previous
height. The faceless being says other things and then,
again, our vision is elevated jerkily. When the faceless
being unclasps us, we see in front of us our body in a bed
with white linens, the man-thing residing in the distance
with a look of feigned concern. Two faceless ones remove
first the linen, peppered with excretions and viscera, and
throw these soiled pieces in a cart nearby, then remove
our clothing. Our sallow yellowed arm and the rest of our
frame appears depleted, a poorly constructed effigy. A
corpse. There is nothing that can return us. The man- thing
in front of us we' ve never known, he' s an imposter.
Herr doppelgänger. It' s a good likeness, although we' ve
never spoken. Yet there it is, refusing to leave our
side. Once the caretakers have finished reapplying the
formaldehdye that keeps us in this petrified state, it will
leave momentarily, then return, carrying a tray laden with
foodstuffs to force down our throat. Taste is an idea long
forgotten. However, the imposter, with the help of the
caretakers, is persistent in prying our jaw open to funnel
a soft, putrid sauce inside us.

When it tires of this task and returns to its seat,
then leaves, the glow masked by the screen recedes into
darkness, and a series of encounters occur. We find
ourselves floating in a room inhabited by a man in white.
It's full of jars containing items we cannot eat. We
hover closeby, but never once is the man in white alerted
to our prescene; it is a relief, for we know we're not
supposed to witness the event. This room, where the man
in white works ceaselesly, is not supposed to exist for
us; it's a scene we've somehow infiltrated. Our forrays
into the forbidden zone are brief, but when we're allowed
to linger, this is what we see: the man in white, slowly
plucking items out of the jars that line every shelf and
corner of the room. There is no visible exit, every area
is overwhelmed with the preserved parts of different
beings, housed in a substance that halts decay and enables
them to be reattached—fully functional—when he deems
it necessary. He is a builder itching at perfection, yet
failing repeatedly. He arranges the items—some familiar,
others unwordly—into outrageous combinations, sewing each
one together, sometimes creating something resembling a
human, others, a strange and hideous chimera, but he's
never satisfied with the end result. He casts the creatures
out, or takes them apart and rearranges them; some become
helpers, others, fodder for the trash heaps from whence they
came. During these visits, we're drawn to understanding
his idea of perfection, for it's well beyond our perception
of the word. He's sculpting new meaning by warping it
into a self-contained, entirely new ideal, poised in frame
with the ancient bone needle, slowly threading through the
sense of things. We know too that somewhere amidst all the
jars in some distant corner sits a piece of ourselves—
our piece—and with each failed being he comes closer
to extracting it, adding it to a history—the one he'll
create with a piece of us—illustrating our future and in

what realm we'll spend eternity, for we are part of his
perfection.

Prior to being interred in the blinding white room we
were situated in a place without doors or windows, with
nothing but empty cupboards. It was there we learned to
starve, and out of doors was always uncomfortable; raining
or snowing, unpleasant and encapsulated in gloom. Before
the imposter, there was the man, robotic in his duties. He
left everyday, to go somewhere, for that we are certain.
But where, and for whom, and to what specific end we've
altogether forgotten by now, or never knew in the first
place. It's unimportant. Soup stretched into every meal,
thinning entirely until becoming nothing more than the idea
of itself. Back then we refused to leave the house, adorned
in shreds and tattered as it was—our frame—for lack of
new clothes, a single solid jacket with which to hide the
filth we were draped in. Of course if you'd have asked
anybody else, they'd tell you we was no worse off than
the next, some even that we were lucky; liars, all of them.
Our troubles began when we were thrown from the train: from
that day forward, we began to disappear. It was our hair
that went first. Each day we'd rise to find more and more
thatches come away in the brush until nothing but a few
stubborn patches remained, dry and coarse like straw. But
when we were thrown from the train—I say we, but really I
mean myself—we were damaged. It's been ever since then,
our problems. Spent everything on a cure, but found none.
The doctors emptied our pockets and exacerbated our claims
by their disingenuous profferings and good cheer, when they
easily read our future suffering in the tattered leaves of
clothing with which we painted our diminishing frames. They
just shook us by the pants till every penny hit the floor,
but he was more naïve, so we had quite a time of it. No

wonder he was so easily replaced. The thing in front of us
now—wherever we are—was beside us when our teeth began
to fall out. There was a day when I suspected something,
but was too afraid to say. We each selected a pair of boots
to be boiled, along with the belts we had; that and a few
handfuls of grass and some salt begged from neighbors.
Shortly afterwards I plucked my teeth out one by one. Most
were rotted anyways. But a few, the ones anchored far in the
back, were big, white and shiny, like the light reflecting
off a serpant' s hide.

Once all the teeth had left us the imposter nestled in.
I' d seen him beforehand, roundabout the area. I stayed
quiet about it at first, unsure whether it was just a
vision, or something that' d pass, like the headaches.
But I' d see him sneaking about the shack, disappearing
around a corner after I' d just come outside. I' d make
chase, but it was always too late. The bugger was quicker
than I could account for. I began to think he was messing
with us somehow. I' d woke one morning to find half a cord
of wood missing. I spoke up about it and my partner said
he' d loaned it to our neighbors, who were too elderly
to chop their own. I started suspecting then that he' d
already been replaced. For safe keeping, I saved our teeth
in jars by the windowsill. One day I walked by the window
and noticed mine were missing. I suspected something foul
and confronted him about it. He said: don' t you remember?
Remember what? I asked. You took them out and buried them,
he said, to grow a tooth plant in the yard. Can you believe
that? The thought of such a thing, and that he had the
brass bedposts to suggest I' d come up with it is absurd.
Where did I bury them? I shouted. He shrugged and went
out and didn' t return until well after dark. He stole my
teeth. They hold a sort of power—things like that do—and
he spent the evening working some strange machinations to
further our deterioration, or hasten it rather. When he
came home I was waiting to confront him. I asked him where
he was and what he was doing. It was all too easy to see
the mask he wore—it tore so easily—came away beneath
our fingernails without resistance. We were unable to
help ourselves. Shrieking, he did his best to cover his
face with his hands but the damage was done; that poorly
made pink and pockmarked mask couldn' t have convinced a
child of its authenticity. If we' d had our teeth we would
have bit him once or twice for good measure. He managed
to run away and lock himself in the pantry—hiding like a

frightened rabbit—from which he didn' t emerge for several
days. I screamed at him through the door, for I was still
angry. I didn' t have any regrets, although I have to admit
his act was quite convincing. Throughout the duration of
his stay in the pantry I remained near the door in case
he made an effort to escape. But I lapsed in vigilance
one evening and when I awoke, he, or it, was gone. At
that point I thought it best to get the law involved and
called to make a report, but the imbecilic operator kept
placing me on hold, asking to repeat myself. After a few
minutes of back and forth we' d given up entirely and simply
screamed, our partner has been replaced, then slammed the
handset down in fury. Several minutes later a group of men
burst through the door. I explained the imposter had fled,
but they seemed unable to understand me. It' s out there
somewhere, I shouted, gesturing with my hands. It was then
I realized, in all the commotion, I' d forgotten to wash: a
thick particulate of skin, hair and blood was caked beneath
our fingernails. The men didn' t seem interested in what I
had to say. I was too weak to put up much of a fight when
they fell upon me and wrapped me up into a sort of plastic,
then transported me to the death chamber.

This blinding whiteness consumes us, devouring our
individuality. It is insurmountable. Unable to move, our
history is slowly usurped. What is a day once passed if you
are dead? We remain stationary at all times, in wonder of
the light. We haven' t the signals necessary to make our
requests heard. These faceless beings make it impossible.
There are occasions where it seems we' ve approached some
sort of understanding—they mutter and walk away, then
return, moving our stiff and yellow body this way and that,
reapplying the death solution to prevent us from further
decay. A plastic doll interred in the house of the infirm.

When we leave off conciousness to observe the architect
we' re also on display: the living pass through slowly and
curiously to catch a small glimpse of the living dead in
the room where we' re installed. The glowing orb the only
sense of the passing of things. Without it we' d be locked
in neverending light or darkness while our face is shoveled
with bittersweet slop. Somewhere far back is a recognition
that twins us with the memory of taste—this taste, the
one in the room—but it' s too diminished. Only an idea of
unpleasantness. How can the dead taste, you ask, to which I
can only reply in answer that we haven' t all the answers,
solely the story by which we' ve lived and died. There' s
a scraping all around us: the orb dims and we' re left with
a blur behind the white screen, the color of the room, the
same as the pieces of cloth which coat our septic limbs.
We remain frozen, sending signals into the ether, the
transistor of the dead acting upon its own accord. There
is again a looming presence, a featureless face where the
features of the face should be. A thin slice of flesh for
the mouth, resembling the shape of an O, slightly recessed
like the top of a pudding cup, as if one could easily
punch it open, or shove their fingers through it to find
a pink tongue to grip, two rows of teeth, transistors in
great contrast to our rotting limbs, which retain a soft,
greenish-yellow hue to play the live bark' s absence. The
nasal cavity of the featureless beings nothing more than
a pixelated blur, the imagining of form coming slowly into
focus, walking in and out of our field of vision before
we' re able to adjust to the image completely. The sallow
glow of our interment echoing as the orb recedes, leaving
us alone with our imposter, donning a new mask after we
shredded the last one they' d given him to bits.

The orb lessens its glow, receding back into its singular reality. We can see the workshop now, even as we speak, or think rather, or whatever the manner in which our thoughts are organized. Surrounded by the pickled members of a thousand species sits the architect of reality, bone needle poised, feverishly composing a new set of coordinates, precisely placing each piece before activation. The area where he is encapsulated thrums with a vibrant greenish glow, jars leave their places on the shelves and float before him, hovering there until, upon closer inspection, he realizes they don't contain the items he needs and he sends them back to their darkened corners. Somewhere on those racks is a piece of us, the only living piece that survives. It was taken to his workshop after being sliced away. In darkness, the architect sends out helpers who scour the human waste of old folks homes and hospitals, extracting parts and specimens before the staff carts them off in secret to the rendering plants. When they cut away my rotten parts they spoke as if doing me a favor, they said they'd found a growth that couldn't be extracted without removing the entirety of my chest. So one day my partner—this was prior to his replacement—dragged me to the house of the infirm and they cut off my tits.

We watch as the architect moves closer and closer to our nasty bits. He sorts through each floating member in front of him like it's a puzzle game on a touch screen, getting closer and closer. The place where our pieces once were has begun to throb, to pulsate beneath our dirty sheets. We remain unable to look down and see for ourselves, but take comfort in the knowledge that soon it will begin to glow and spread, this toxic light emanating from where they cut us up and sewed us back together again. It's undulating, like a shockwave in the deep ocean. We can feel it and it feels

good to feel after so long. It's traveling and powerful.
The architect reaches for one jar, taps it with the tip of
his finger, sends it back into the noxious green shade of
the limb shelves. How does he leave this place, we wonder,
as there seems to be no exit. It seems as though he never
ceases work, so it's possible he never leaves. But the
beings he constructs and casts aside are sent upon errands
in the night, so there must be a way. Our body shakes and
judders. We float above his work bench, eyes peeled. The
architect twists the cap loose of one of the jars in front
of him, letting its contents spill out upon the slick steel
operating table. The room in white grows ever blinding as
our body sheds its layers. The faceless beings approach
and begin force feeding us with the garbage sauce. Upon
the architect's table is a revelation. Amidst the glop
and goo that housed the piece is the one they've taken
from us. We watch as the architect slowly and carefully
lifts one, plying its softness, passing it from one hand
to the other. He picks up the other piece of us, lying
on the table, the slickness of which glints softly in the
gaseous light. The architect holds our cancerous breasts
in his hands, as the faceless ones ram a feeding tube down
our throat and pump gallons of applesauce into our mouth.
He stitches the two breasts together, making them whole
again, and places them there in a corner of the table. The
architect leans back and cracks his oversized knuckles and
the faceless beings continue pumping their bittersweet
compound deep inside our dead gut. The architect recedes
from vision now, leaving us in awe, wondering what he will
sew our cancerous breasts onto and how to escape from this
raunchy palace of the dead. This light inside us continues
to grow, glowing outwards and scorching all of our captors
with a sallow brilliance like that of septic child. A
thought freezes the faceless being ramming our face full
of sauce and a low, guttural scream issues forth from

somewhere inside it, growing in frequency until the small
flap of flesh covering their **O** mouth vibrates like an ear
drum. The architect pauses for a moment over his work,
then continues. The skin covering the **O** mouth burns away,
spreading apart like a single spark igniting a thin strip
of film. **O** the O it's spreading wider and wider, consuming
the faceless features of the One before us until, with a
final shuddering and cracking, all we see before us is an
Open p**O**rtal in varying shades of darkness, undulating
to match the frequency of our once-cancerous chest while
the architect elsewhere fingers and sews **O**ur breasts onto
something wh**O**lly different. We vibrate violently and can
feel **O**urselves, pieces, being broken apart, an essence
being sucked into the p**O**rtal in front of us, dissolving
atomic particles being filtered from **O**ne reality to the
next, and in this m**O**ment, **O**ur vision fades and dissolves
as our final particulate is c**O**nsumed and transp**O**rted into
the darkened frontal v**O**id space.

Zone 2:

A Trip to the Emergency Room: Our Way & the Arm Follows, Or
The Valley of the Phantom Lim)b)p

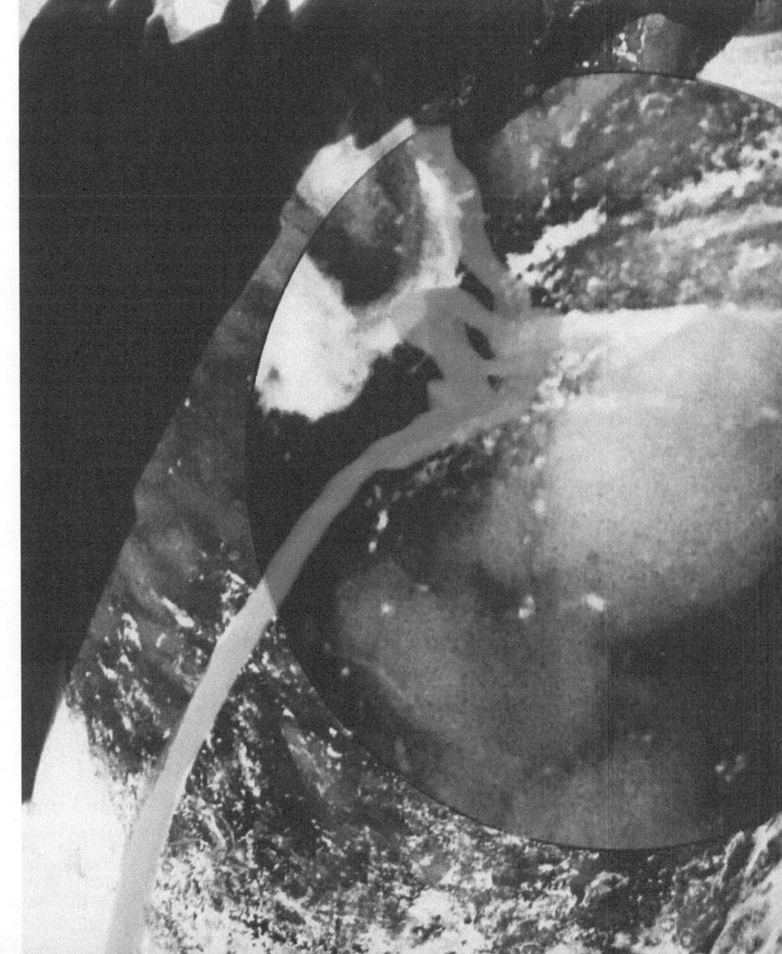

the blue ball is below the bed you are there
the blue ball is below the bed BELOW THE BED
BELOW THE BED BELOW THE BED BELOW THE BED
four metal arms beneath us
we can see it but we can't reach it held up like water, or
like in the water
THE BLUE BALL IS BELOW THE BED
it's a ball not a balloon or is it a balloon? no
no it's a ball
white walls and nothing, a white nothing, like the ball
floats inside A BLUE BALL
like outside it's grey and the valley is frozen
in the valley you exist, but different, like in time
frozen in the hardness of the valley where it all falls
apart where the people fall beneath us
ground into things into US

the sky in the valley is different; not blue like the BALL
UNDER THE BED

why aren' t you here yet? are you here yet? you were
following us when we came in like always just outside
perhaps now there' s no one else except the ball: it is the
only thing it floats here with us, and the four shiny posts
beneath our respite, it' s nice to be on a cloud for a while
US AND THE BALL I' m shouting THE BLUE BALL BENEATH THE
BED & ONLY US & THE BALL why aren' t you here? you were
behind us since the valley, which is what we remember, just
outside you said when they wheeled us out and down the hall
you couldn' t come but we' d be fine because, they' re only
helping then you' d be right outside...RIGHT OUTSIDE but
we' re in front, always first so you can see us from there
where you are in darkness or waiting or outside in the
frozen day we feel we could write something but we can' t
and they' ll have to teach us how to do it over cause now I
can' t feel it anymore or I can feel the arm but it' s not
there and that I' m sleeping and when I wake up it won' t
be like it was before they rolled me into the hall ARE YOU
STILL THERE? did you see us when we went by, did you see
how they' ve taken the piece away?
they said it would make the perfect fit
I' m shouting out loud but there' s nothing now the BALL
BELOW not the THE BED BALL BELOW THE BED A BLUE ONE...A BLUE
BALL BELOW THE BED
you were just going to be gone and come back but maybe they
won' t let you in and you really are right outside
IS EVERYTHING RIGHT OUTSIDE?
Outside where we once were, where we came from, us first
and then your forever following backwards.

the way it was when we came in was like when smoke gets in
your eyes...you were shouting at all the people dressed
in white about IT TOOK THE VALLEY IT TOOK THE VALLEY but
what took the valley I don' t know but maybe that' s where
you went to see if what you thought had tooken it really
did take it or if there' s more of it left to take but THE
VALLEY IS GONE OR IF IT ISN' T EVEN YOU' RE JUST OUTSIDE
BRING SOMETHING WITH YOU, OUCH
I think it' s there and then gone again, the arm

we' re with the ball below the bed and you' re right
outside we cannot move and we' re going to die
YOU SAID ROADKILL THEY TOOK THE VALLEY IT TOOK THE VALLEY
call me roadkill sleeping
call me roadkill placed upon the riverbank to crumble like
the rest of them call me roadkill and rot away like our past
we see a place where my arm used to be but wrapped like a
package; like the way they keep to hide something I COULD
HEAR YOU IF YOU WERE JUST OUTSIDE
did you go to the valley to see?
did you find the part of me that' s missing? did you see it?
we look now and close our eyes and imagine waxpaper and
something bound with string like we' ve bought it from
somewhere long ago in time.

I AM ABOVE THE BLUE BALL BELOW THE BED...I am in the BED
you are just outside and sleeping with my eyes close I know
I' m sleeping because my eyes are close and if I were just
resting it would be different
THEY TOOK THE SMOKE IN THE VALLEY can you hear it when I do
that? I can in my head, like it bounces of the wall like in
the valley when you shout across it WHAT DID THEY TAKE?
nothing but grey air and people trees to watch the water' s

sparkling I wish you were next to me in there, next to
us, but don' t touch me WHEN I OPEN MY EYES AGAIN WE' LL
BE GONE don' t touch me watch me fall away, crumble into
nothing time is what makes us and the valley eats its people
trees

last week walking when I fell and got a cut I can feel it
now but I feel it on us not where away it' s in the valley
or somewhere else WHY CAN I FEEL SOMETHING IT ISN' T THERE?
it' s on the part they took from us but before I came here
I close my eyes because they were burning now if I open them
again I' ll remain here you' ll be just outside but me and
the arm will be placed in a box A BOX AND A BLUE BALL BELOW
THE BED FAR BELOW WHERE THE GROUND GETS SOFTY

they took to tinker with it and see what doors it opens,
that' s what they said, they said if I didn' t like it it
was fine because I wasn' t what they wanted anyways, but
our piece could contain a perfect message, one we' ve been
groomed all days to tell, one that' s kept us traveling our
history through the greyish valley where everything' s the
same but different. this place where there is no night, but
day is never bright enough.

When they took me down the white lady told me I' d have a
phantom limp to feel where my arm went. Is that the way
then? like the other pieces before ours they feel it where
it is when it' s gone and somewhere else.

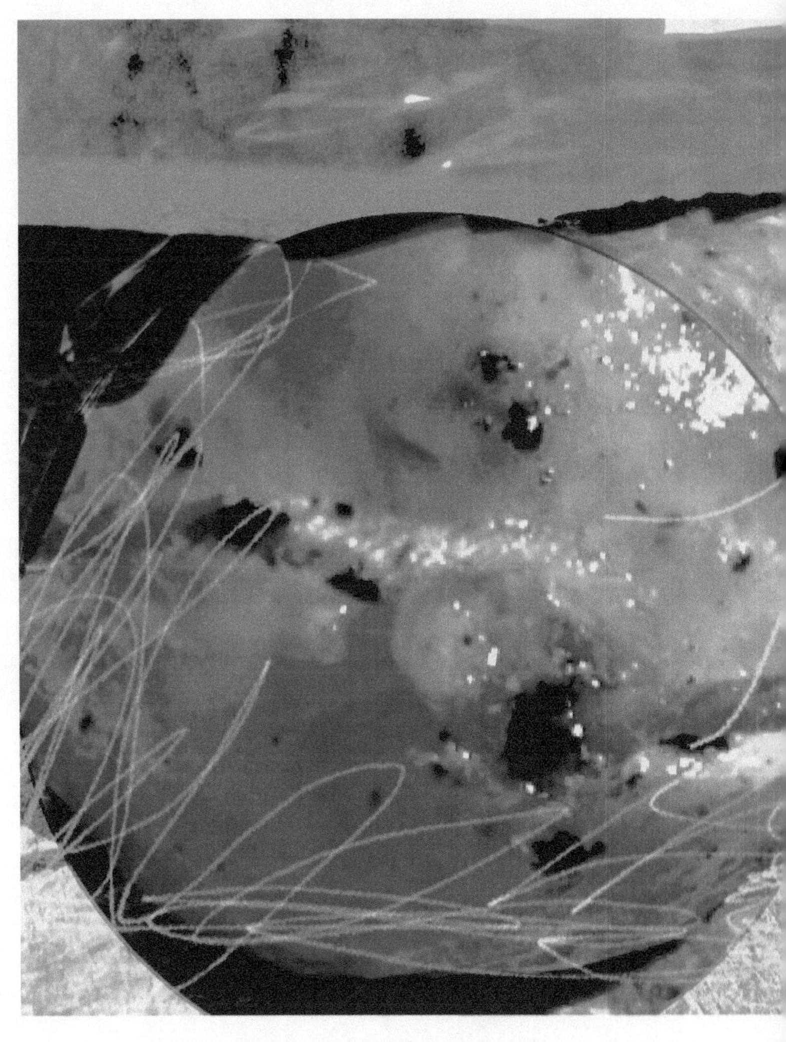

A PHANTOM LIMP IS LIKE A GHOST BUT FOR A PIECE OF US
THAT'S RUN AWAY

you went to look for it, didn't you? you said I was the
key and that you'd protect it, or me or whatever piece of
us was the one to unlock it, so you must be there to find

it for us but now you' ve left us alone again, we feel your
absence like the arm. even if you found it, it wouldn' t
matter because it would still be a phantom lip anyways
a man in white comes in now where we' re sleeping, or I am,
somewhere else my arm is planted in the earth like a tree
the fingers stretch out and point in different directions
toward smoke but not fire or fire then smoke SMOKE THEN
FIRE THEN SMOKE the man in the room is dressed like a doctor
but smells like death. are you a doctor if you can' t save
a thing from dying?

a small flashlight in his hand and opens our right eye our
left eye we' re backwards all the eyes SMOKE and grey we
begin to fade and find ourselves amidst the bentback trees
again, the wind whipping rotten things toward us as we
trudge through mush, the river always on our left.

it was this way always when we were together, or you chased
me and caught me, before they' d removed what we held dear,
or had been groomed to hold, that piece of flesh bearing
fragile fingers.

second eye other eye watch our fingers stretch to the
greyish ceiling, the soft sky open it up we try and wave to
where our friends, our memories might have gone, to you,
where you' re searching for us as well, or the part you
most desire. THE BLUE BALL REMAINS BELOW OUR HAND CLAWS FOR
NOTHING

a whole body like a phantom lip that' s how I am we' re
here but I' m like a phantom lip if smoke arrives before
a fire then the ground gets soft. it' s like I can feel
we' re back there but here as well. this man is not a
doctor, he is interested in our specimen, but where he took
it there' s a wall of history, like an all star jam; that
just popped in and out, no idea.

IN THE VALLEY THERE' S AN ARM WITH FINGER BRANCHES WHERE
THERE BUT ALSO HERE PART OF US INSTALLED smoke is lots of
things like when there' s fire or tears or the sky' s not
morning not night, like sleeping when it' s neither dark
nor light, like we remember it.

there were times you pushed us and times you chased us but
we knew somehow there was both love and danger, or the
power of both propelling (a nurse comes in now and unwraps
our present and we see it even though it' s not supposed to
like the end of a frankfurter tied with a string YUCK)

The nurse sticks a needle and there's a twitch THE MAN
TRIES TO OPEN OUR EYES MAKE HIM STOP YOU'RE RIGHT OUTSIDE
MAKE HIM STOP COME IN FROM THERE TO HELP US OR the man is
a doctor because of the thing around his neck no one but
doctors have those things around their necks we're still
sleeping but every time he shines the light we fade and pass
through but we're afraid of returning, we haven't grown
yet enough to return.

why have you left us? why have you planted these items
and walked away? once we were together like a part of
ourselves, you told me it was necessary to continue, but
now towards where? if they drop us off along the bank again
will we crumble like the rest of them? We're afraid we'll
crumble. how could you let that happen to us?

the lady in white throws the needle in the trash and says
it so we can't hear but maybe we're really somewhere
else LIKE YOU WE'RE RIGHT OUTSIDE take me before they can
take me but no it's too late already the woman the nurse
is using her foot to move the wheels and the doctor takes
the thing from off his neck and places it on our chest then
places it back around his neck like a scarf and picks up
the end where our head is we think we feel a jolt and he
slides it away from the wall and we're moving now we pass
a village of walls and other pieces and it's like we've
bled through here and there, as it dims we follow it like
a maze. ARE YOU OUTSIDE? WHAT ELSE IS OUTSIDE? WILL YOU
SEE US THEY MAYBE ARE TAKING US TO YOU NOW YOU ARE WAITING
RIGHT OUTSIDE WE ARE WAITING RIGHT OUTSIDE we watch the
blue ball kicked into a corner as the man doctor pushes us
away holding the bed and thing around his neck to keep from
sliding off but now we're looking down and in the room and

there' s the ball its color is wrong like it was left in the
sun too long and fading now it doesn' t work and there are
noises outside the room we try to go there and it' s like
it left us or we don' t know, like pushing through a wet
sheet, we just can' t, the ball isn' t moving but it isn' t
where it used to be when they took us it must have rolled
or been hit by the wheel or the nurse or the doctor with
the thing around his neck when they were wheeling us and
now the blue ball isn' t below anything but itself because
there' s nothing now there' s nothing now in the room and
we feel different, it' s there but floating in darkness
and fading, but somehow the black is shiny, like a pair of
gloves they' d given us once.

WE' RE RUNNING AWAY CAN YOU FEEL US DID WE ROLL BY YOU JUST
OUTSIDE IS A WHOLE BODY A PHANTOM LIP? They couldn' t find
the piece of us they wanted, now we know this, because it
wasn' t a part of us like that, or it was inside of us, but
impossible for them to properly extract. We are floating in
a pool of shiny black gloves, tapping upon each finger a
horrible moment. Abandonment, pain and ladies clothing, or
what we wore in the dark; ephemera. it all seems so short
now and realizing that to exist only as a child grown to be
torn into pieces.

as we watch the blue ball continues to get lighter the room
is too bright to look at we try to raise our arm to block
it but it isn' t where we left it then the room is all
white now, or almost the blue ball even is disappearing,
like fading once the room is gone we' ll be somewhere else
once the room is gone where we' ll be is elsewhere but
everywhere too we think ARE YOU THERE?

we can' t remember the white hurts to see even with a
phantom lip it shines too hard the room is gone we see a sky
filled with smoke on one part and another side it' s blue
like the ball but not it sounds like rain but it isn' t
raining but we can hear it in front of us is our arm, like
it was before the valley but in the valley now we think,
we' re in the valley with it maybe the arm is in the middle
and splits the sky to blue and grey like rain but not rain
it' s piercing us somehow but we can' t see where it' s
coming from and we can' t look away WE TURN OUR HEAD BUT
THE ARM FOLLOWS if you' re still outside then you' re far
away and we' re alone but they took the valley so some
might be coming to find us if we' re here THEY TOOK THE
VALLEY THEY TOOK THE VALLEY THEY TOOK THE VALLEY HELP HELP
ME ARE YOU NEAR HELP ME WHO TOOK THE VALLEY DOES IT MATTER
WHERE YOU ARE IS WHERE I COULD BE BUT WE' RE BOTH JUST
OUTSIDE THE ROOM when I move my head the arm follows and
the noise gets louder like rain and it grows darker and the
ball-like blue in the sky follows grey then black something
behind us try to turn but the arm follows turn our head
but the arm follows the noise like rain now it' s sand we
know and the arm follows and we feel it even though it' s
a phantom lip the arm follows in front up to the elbow in
sand and like it' s raining and the sky all black and the
wind is strong and flakes of things floating in the air and
the wind WHERE ARE YOU THEY' VE TAKEN OUT THE STRING AND
TRIED TO and the wind is stronger and stronger the air full
of flakes the black sky and flashes we turn to something
shaking us the arm follows sand stings our phantom lip like
waving out of the car window during a thunderstorm and in
this world everything is born to be harvested the night
black...00o.

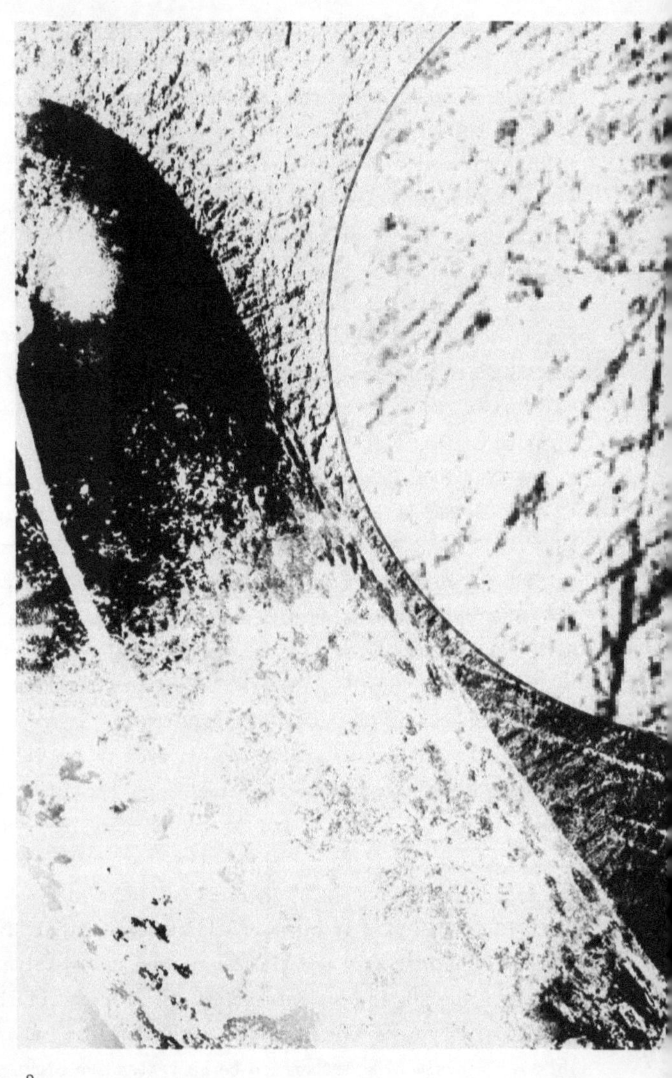

Zone 3:

The Fly & the Poet / Cavernous Exile & Wings

*Tell me about the beginning...describe it to me, to the
best of your ability.*

At first, there was nothing. It was...there was nothing. In
one sense, it was darkness. There was no light. No feeling.
But there was awareness that something was...that we could
communicate with ourselves. Something deeper, but aside
from feeling. Awareness at a more primordial level. More
like that we knew that there was something more than there
was...that it just hadn' t happened yet...that...it' s
difficult to describe.

Do your best.

It' s difficult to describe because what I' m describing
is feeling, but it wasn' t feeling in that sense. We felt
nothing...there was nothing. But some sort of connection
that I think only now I can put my finger on because it was
unlike anything...because we were nothing, or we hadn' t
been able to hatch, or to be born yet. But there was
something else. There was something...it was something else.
And looking back on it, it was a connection. And although
it was dark and we couldn' t feel anything, it wasn' t
static, what we felt. It was...it was something else. It
was movement in the sense that...that maybe, I don' t know,
that maybe we weren' t alone. Maybe we were together with
something. We were in existence without being in existence
because of this feeling, or not a feeling, but this kind
of connection that was ingrained in us. As if something
more important would develop. And I guess that' s maybe
a way you could think about it at this pre-larval stage.
It was almost akin to some sort of something developing

in the full sense...in the sense of the word as we went
through the larval stages but also as um...as kind of as...
for example, take a photo. A photo needs to be developed
in order for us to see what the film holds. And when it
starts, it's empty. It's potential...everything in a
vacuum. There's darkness but intent. And then suddenly
it's burned with an image, and then washed and the image
is urged out and enlarged and becomes something...it becomes
something, becomes a picture. But in the beginning there's
all this potentiality there that...it's like a wheel
waiting to roll. That's the best way I can describe, aside
from the photography analogy. It's like a wheel waiting to
roll, but it hasn't begun yet. But the fact that it's a
wheel makes us expect something more.

Tell me about the hatching.

The hatching took place over what seemed...to be reflecting
upon it now...what seemed to be a vast stretch of time.
Although, I imagine it took place over a matter of weeks,
or days. I'm not sure exactly the science behind it. But
it seemed like forever because...because it was such a
subtle happening. Uh...one moment we were in that stage
I described earlier...waiting for the wheel to turn, so
to speak, that stage of anticipation. And then we were
free. But in between that...in between those two moments,
looking back on it now, there was very, very, very subtle
changes, that were unnoticeable at the time. Much...I
don't know...I mean, in the way that a plant grows perhaps
...(*inaudible*)...Um, and you can't see by looking at
it...you can't...I mean you can watch it grow but unless
there's a way to mark it somehow, visually I guess, at
certain increments of time, it would appear as though it
wasn't growing at all, until you reflected back on it.
And that's the way it was. The hatching was just kind of
completed when it was completed. We didn't realize there
was a process going on behind it. But, as I mentioned,
there were these subtle, subtle changes that I only realize
now looking back on it, which were indications of what was
happening. The wheels speeding up, the plant growing, the
photo in the silver bromide solution, or what have you.
And these indicators were primarily light and temperature.
Things slowly came into focus...or became lighter, as if...
well, as if someone was removing the bandages of somebody
who had just recently had eye surgery or something...
you know, you're supposed to remove them slowly so the
eyes can acclimate themselves, or re-acclimate themselves
to light again, to the brightness of it. And...and so,
it was the same for us in a lot of ways. Because we were

tender then, you know? The larval stages are very tender
times. And it's something that isn't rushed, because if
it's rushed, or it ends too early, death, I mean there's
only death. Because the larva can't survive because
of...I don't know...I guess what's out there beyond the,
beyond the sac once they break through. So we were slowly
acclimated to some sort of...some light...things began to
brighten slowly. Like I said it wasn't anything that we
could perceive at that moment because it was (*inaudible*)...

When I say light though, you have to keep in mind that...
you have to keep in mind the minute degree that I'm talking
about. Because at this point, we were still below deck.

We were in the hold. We could sense this change in light,
but it was so minute...and when I say there were indications
that things were happening, there were also noises, but it
was all very indescribable because it was something that
we couldn' t...we had no...well number one we were insects,
or we didn' t have any sense of what the world was. I mean
we had a sense of what was vaguely happening. But at that
stage, there were noises, there were sounds, there were
pulsations almost, things like echoes that must have been
produced by wherever the ship was going at that point, or
where...storms or waves or something, I don' t know. There
were vibrations I guess that...they were a deep sort of
rumbling that again, we didn' t pay any attention to really
because it was...it was so foreign and indescribable. And
it didn' t affect us as much as the other factors did; the
change in temperature, the subtlety of the light and so
forth.

Tell me about those changes...

The temperature changes were weird, because, for the most
part when we were inside the...when we hadn' t broken
through yet and we were, you know in the kind of gestation
period, it seemed rather warm and then slowly, slowly
over time, again changes much in the same way that the
light changed, the subtlety of the light, it began to
get cooler...the temperatures began to become a bit more
extreme until...again, it was like, once we realized what
was happening, we were already free. We were out, you know?
Amidst everything...it was the final...well I guess not the

final part of the larval stage but once we broke through we
were outside of the egg and could move about freely and it
was completely different. And...it was...it was wonderful.
The larval stage was one of the most singularly enjoyable
events I've ever experienced.

Why was it wonderful? In what sense?

I mean breaking out...or finding ourselves out was
wonderful. Because at that stage, I guess nearing the
end of the larval stage, or in the middle, once we were
outside, once we had broken free, there was only one
thing that we paid attention to and that was this kind of
insatiable hunger unlike anything I've...anything I could
compare it to.

Um...what was so unique about it was being born and then experiencing this insatiable hunger while simultaneously... basically...living in a world that you could eat. We were in a world that...that was all...we could eat it. We could eat. And we could continue to eat. And we did so until there was nothing left. But for so long, that was the only thing that we knew, the only thing we paid attention to was the drive to feed and gorging ourselves and that need never really going away. And then all of a sudden it was...our world was gone, because we'd eaten it all. And of course what I'm speaking of is the...the...where we hatched, which was, I don't know, a dead goat, or sheep or lamb or something, one of the animals that had died on the way over and we ate it all. We were born, and then ate it. And once that was gone it was on to the next stage, which was basically the end of the larval stage and the beginning of something entirely different. So after we had eaten our whole world, so to speak, there was a long...or what seemed like a long and endless period of hibernation. Another gestation period before we became the swarm.

Somewhat, but it was distinct. This gestation period was... it was the same, but not. It seemed to pass much quicker, although we weren't really aware as much of the passage of time. It was really much more of a hibernation and gestation period than the first part because in the first part we were aware of the slight changes of light and

temperature, but this time around things were much thicker.
But after an indeterminate amount of time, we were released
and then we took to the air. And as I said earlier, we
were in the ship's hold. So when we took to the air, we
were in the hold and at first it was hard to make out what
else was in the hold with us, but after a time we figured
out that there was stuff to eat, of course eating now was
completely different as well. But there was...there was an
abundance of food and we kind of had the run of the place.
It was filled with mostly animals. Some crew members slept
there at night but they were the worst of the lot...rough
drunks, or the guys that got into fights. And when I say
eating was completely different I mean that...really...I
mean the hunger was there but...also...the manner in which
we ate was different. Because earlier on we basically had,
in the larval stage we had pincers and now it took much
more work to eat. Because we had to prepare our meals,
so to speak. What I mean by this of course is...I mean I
don't know if you know...you might have some idea of how
a fly eats, it has to essentially vomit this compound onto
what it plans to eat to break it down into something it can
digest...I think it was mostly digestive fluids. To begin
the digestions before we consumed it. But the hold was a
dark, very dirty and smelly place, because it was full of
the excrement and expectorations of all the animals that
were being held there. And there were a lot of them. Of
course we loved it. Lambs, goats, sheep, horses...even dogs
and cats. Things that were meant to feed an entire crew
for an extended period at sea, in addition to, once the
crew arrived at their intended destination...the crew, or
whoever they were...to continue raising these animals for
sustenance. But we were just...we just flew around and laid
on the piles of shit and ate what we could find. It was
so simple, at that point. There wasn't much else to do.
We struggled to find a way to go beyond the hold and out

into the open air. After some time a situation presented
itself to me and at one point I left the rest of the swarm
behind and went beyond the door and out into the ocean air.
And that was something...something else, because I wasn't
really prepared for, number one the amount of...of the
force of wind that they were experiencing at the time and
the second I got out of the door I was blown away, hundreds
of feet into the air. I kind of watched this magnificent
ship beneath me kind of disappear before my eyes as I was
blown into the atmosphere. And it took me...it was quite
some time before I could descend and find my way back to
the deck again.

*Were you ever aware that you were unlike the rest of the
swarm, or the others you were with?*

Not at first, because as I mentioned, we spent much of our
time down in the hold in the darkness. It wasn't until we
reached land that I realized I was like the rest of the
swarm, in the sense that I was part of the swarm, thought
like them, but I became aware...slightly aware...that I
could identify these things due to possibly...I suppose the
previous associations I had had with them at one time or
another. For example, when we were in the cave I knew...
not knew...I didn't really know what anything was—not
definitively—but I knew that I recognized some things.
There was a familiarity that made me kind of think—of
course this is all very out there and vague and ambiguous
because I had no capacity to think like a normal human
being—but there was still some sort of recognition and
most of it came through when I heard certain words being
spoken; that's when I most felt like I was something else.
The sound and the effect that the sound of certain words

had on me...I mean it had an effect on me...the rest of the
swarm paid no mind because it was insubstantial. There was
only eating and procreating and trying to stay alive. So
it makes no sense that a certain tonality of a word being
spoken, or something like that would generate any sort of
recognition. But for me it did and I was unsure as to why.
Because at that moment I didn' t really have the capacity
to remember things; like I heard the word...I don' t know,
"sun," and then remembered: oh yes, the sun is the thing
that...it' s the ball that circles the earth, or that gives
light to the darkness, or the day. It wasn' t anything like
that. But when a word was spoken I would immediately prick
my ears up, in a manner of speaking. And of the course the
person that was speaking was the Poet. There weren' t many
visitors at that time. We were in a really remote area,
quite desolate. But the swarm loved it. Feeding off of the
animals that were attracted to the salt water. It was the
perfect place for us. But I was always drawn toward the
interior of the Cave because I thought there was something
special about it. I thought that it was different so I
stayed as close as I could. Waiting for those tiny pieces
of recognition.

At this point I'd like to try a little experiment if that's alright?

Experiment?

*Yes. If it's alright with you I'd like to try to bring
you back there for a moment. Can I do that?*

Alright, if you think it will help.

I do.

OK then.

Wonderful...

Now, I'd like you to close your eyes for a moment. That's it. Now breathe deeply, almost in an exaggerated manner. Yes. Concentrate on the sound of your breathing, focus all of your energy on it. Imagine that it's not your breath, but the steady wash of the waves upon the shore. Imagine it's the tide coming in, slowly, bringing you back... that's it... back to where you once were.

Now, I'm going to count backwards from five, and when I reach the number one, you will open your eyes and be back there, ready?

five...

four...

three...

two...

one...

*Now, can you hear me...nod if you can hear me... Good.
Now take a deep breath. Look around you. Can you tell me
where you are?*

I'm in the cave.

Which cave?

The cave by the sea.

What do you see?

The Poet.

I can see him many times over. He sits far away, in front
of me. There's a tallow candle nearby him, the only other
light source save for the minute amount coming in through
the entrance.

The air is salty. I can taste it.

I see him many times, but he moves as one. Slowly. I'm
attracted to the light from the candle so I approach him but
I'm blown back by the intensity of the heat it exudes.

I anchor myself on a nearby wall to watch, moving sparingly
so he's unable to detect our presence.

At this point we can't make out what he's writing; he
mumbles to himself, unintelligibly.
Now I'm aware, I understand.

What are you aware of?

I'm different from the rest of them. I catch bits and
pieces of language. The sound of the wind blowing by the
hole to the cave.

What of this sound?

It is something I recognize. It vibrates within, creating
a whistling as it drags by, pushing the flame of the candle
this way and that like a lung.

The Poet sits in front of us doing the same thing over
and over again, mumbling to himself. Scraping upon the
parchment.

I can't read it.

Try to...

I cannot

Why?

I don' t want to look. He' ll notice me.

What else do you see?

The livestock.
He keeps them and the servants slaughter them one by one,
salting the pieces and burying them in clay pots.

He' s afraid no one will come for him.

How do you know?

We can smell his desperation.

What about desperation?

The Cave reeks of it, it' s permeated with the stench of
desperation, much like the smell of a frightened animal.

He' s frightened?

Undoubtedly. But he does not show it. He hides behind
words.

How does he hide behind words?

By exercising metaphor to skirt their true meaning.

Can you give me an example?

The shadows on the wall. He plies meanings from them that
are imprecise.

How are they imprecise?

Because they are shadows.

What is he writing?

He's writing an opus to the dead. A last gasp at
forgiveness that will fall upon deaf ears, for what he's
done is unforgivable, because he's done nothing but become
himself, performed his duty.

I don't understand. Help me to understand.

He is the Poet who's been cast out after his usefulness
has come to an end. He's been drained and cast aside like
an empty wineskin tossed into the gutter.

Who has tossed him aside?

The Great Philosopher King.

In a city founded by wolves came the Great Philosopher
King, who ushered his children out of darkness and into a
blinding light. But only for a time.
Only for a time.

Do you mean the city of Rome?

Rome was only an idea; the true city lies beyond its form.

Can you tell me what the Poet writes?

I can tell you what he wants to be heard.

He wants his beloved King to take him back into the graces,
but they will not. The Poet wants to sculpt a new philosophy
in which forgiveness is mandatory and he cannot. The Poet
is as useless as the shadows which surround him, as fleeting
as when the candlelight' s extinguished.

I don't understand.

Of course you don't understand, for you're a shadow.

How do you mean I am a shadow, in what sense?

In the sense that you are indirect. You are circling the
flame when what you really want is to go straight through
it, to be blinded with answers. But if you traveled this
route the questions you'd be left with would burn your eyes
out.

How could one be blinded by answers?

Indeed. It perhaps is difficult to understand, but when
questions reach a truth too great, inexplicable in its
immensity, then all perception is lost. All sense is
distorted. Meaning can only go so far, understanding as
well, in elucidation. For what is an answer if the truth is
so blinding it obliterates the question?

*I'm sorry but you've lost me. Could we perhaps return to
the Cave and the Poet?*

You are feeble-minded herr doctor. You waste our time with
senseless questions. It is tiring even for us, who have been
awake for centuries.

...

(At this point the patient refused to continue speaking and
the session was terminated. But it seems, at first glance,
it was a remarkable success. We may continue using the same
method in subsequent sessions. Moving forward, I'd like
to gain additional insight into the intentions of the Poet
in addition to, perhaps, the state and intentions of the
observer, or, as the patient calls themselves, the Fly.
There may even be more undiscovered alternate personalities
deeper inside the patient's psyche we've yet to reach.)

Good afternoon. How are you feeling today?

Well, thank you.

Wonderful. Again, I' d like to express my gratitude at your willingness to speak with me, as well as allowing several of my colleagues to be present this afternoon. They' ll only be observing.

Of course *(chuckles)* What else would I be doing? Let' s hope I can give them something to see.

Well, I' m sure I' m speaking for everyone when I say that we do hope you' re comfortable and not too maladjusted. I mean, I truly do. I hope that you are putting your free time to good use.

For introspection?

Exactly. Yes! For introspection. This is why we are here today. Knowing yourself is the beginning of all wisdom, as they say.

Ganz ehrlich mit sich selbst zu sein, ist eine gute Übung.

Ah. I' m impressed. But it' s much more than an exercise isn' t it, for us at least?

Perhaps for you. For myself, all horrors lie within.

Yes, well, for the time being perhaps. But we' re here to change all that aren' t we?

I' m here against my will. Whatever I can do to be released I will, within reason. However, I' ve been thinking in all my free time, that perhaps I' ve let you walk around in my mind too much. You' ve rearranged the furniture, so to speak, and now it' s all grown wrong. *(at this point, the patient has stood up and begun pacing the room).*

*How do you mean grown wrong? Please sit down. (I motion
toward the chair in the center of the room.) Try and
relax. All we want to do is help you, so feel free to say
whatever' s on your mind.*

I can' t articulate it precisely.

*Try describing how you feel. Mentally...physically, it
doesn' t matter. Let' s start there.*

I feel you' re trying to rob me of something.

*Well that' s certainly a start. (At this point, one of my
colleagues chuckles, eliciting a hateful glare from the
patient. I ask them politely to leave the room for a time
and they willingly comply).*

My apologies. Please continue.

It' s as if you' re extracting something out of me, robbing
me of something dear. But I can' t identify precisely what
it is, only that it' s painful and something that' s a part
of us.

What do you mean when you say "us"?

You know exactly what I mean doctor.

Perhaps so. But I' d like to hear it from you.

I mean Us. The Fly, the Poet. The Cave even. Everything we are and once were and will become. All that' s inside of us. There' s a film we switch between when we have no place to go.

And this film, is it you, or is it we or us?

It' s everything and nothing.

I' m sorry but I don' t understand. But I have an idea. Perhaps we can do a little exercise to help us navigate this new, unfamiliar territory.

I' m at your mercy herr doctor.

Well don' t say it like that (I chuckle) I' d like to think we' ve come farther in developing our relationship. Don' t you think so?

Perhaps in some ways. I must be in a mood. My apologies, please overlook my sarcasm today and proceed with this exercise. I' m slightly intrigued.

Alright then. I' d like you to draw a map of where these creatures live inside you. In which parts of your body do they reside?

Alright, I shall if you insist? Do you think it could help?

Do you want to be helped? To be cured of your sickness?

Yes... or if not cured then better understand.

That' s good... that' s very good. Here then (at this point I hand him a piece of paper and my fountain pen.)

Shall I?

Go right ahead. (The patient begins etching out some sort of crude image of a man onto the piece of paper we' ve given him. After a moment or so he turns back toward me with a smile.)

Doctor. I don' t mean to be rude but it' s a little difficult to focus with somebody gazing over my shoulder like that.

*Of course, of course. My apologies. I' ll busy myself
elsewhere. (At this point I' ll fast forward a few minutes,
as all that exists is static/the scratching of the pen.
I leave off to rummage around my files. Opening drawers
and removing papers to place upon my desk with no clear
intention...)*

(Several minutes later)

I believe I' ve got something for you to look at now,
Doctor.

Do you then?

Yes, come here. I think you' ll like what you see.

*(I go over to the other side of the room where I was
standing before and try to peer over his shoulder. He moves
in such a way as to obstruct my view.) I' m sorry but I can
quite see with you in the way like that.*

Oh my apologies. I didn' t realize. Here you are. Do you
see now?

Yes, yes I think I do.

Do you see everything?

What do you mean, everything?

Here doctor. You must see it all. You can see it all right there. All of them. Do you see?

I' m not so sure. Let me...

Here you can see it now. It' s there. What do you think? Can you see it? Come closer...

(At this point I squat down onto my haunches and inch towards the patient). But I can' t quite...

There you are. Now you can see all of them. CAN' T YOU SEE.
CAN' T YOU FUCKING SEE YOU DIRTY PEASANT PIG FUCK. ....
YOU SEE. THE THREE. THE VOID THE
EVERYTHING ....

...   .

...   ...

...

*(You're all aware of what happens next. At this point the
patient jams the pen into our neck, puncturing our carotid
artery. He raises his arms back to do so again but at this
point, the orderlies rush in and manage to restrain him
just as his arm brandishing the fountain pen begins to fall.
He is dragged to the other side of the room and sedated.
If it wasn't for our outstanding triage staff, I wouldn't
have survived.)*

Zone 4:

Clinical Lycanthropy / La Bocca Al Lupo

Blow the candle out. Blow the candlelight out and let us fly fly into the night. Blow it up, blow it out. Let us dance and dance no more upon the walls on nothing. Upon the walls of shadow. Let us dance dance into the walls of shadowed night into the air. Let us leave this rotten sanctuary. THIS PISS SOAKED CAVERN. Do you hear me? I know you' re there, watching. Do you hear me. I' m burning. Please have mercy. I call mercy. I regret what I' ve done let me beg for mercy. I' m begging, do you fucking hear me. You' re watching me aren' t you? I can' t leave this corner. This putrid phosphorescence, it burns. You are slowly killing me. You all. Do you have any idea what it' s like? To live in this way. It will come without regard for you, whether you like it or not. It' s going to a world of ours. Everything will cease and then we can start it like it should have been. Once it ceases forever. The ice will burn your exurbs. You won' t want it but you will.

Watch the world fade.

Please. Have mercy. I' m begging. Can' t you see? It' s
never not dark in this horrid room where they' re holding
us. Amidst to glowing we' re slaked with an impenetrable
thirst; a fortress of unsatiated wont. I can tell you all
about them if you could only find it in your hearts to let
me rest. To lower the rays just a little enough to breathe
again. Would that be alright? Could you do that and I' ll
tell you about them. About all of them who' ve ever lived.
About being born and dying. Could you see yourselves to let
us live like that a little, perhaps less blindingly? My god
it' s as if our mouth was stuffed with cotton all the time.

In the corner we' ve found a little spot that' s not so
bright. It' s not dark but maybe so. No. But close to be at
least. In the dark corner it' s close to being dark, shaded
from the phosphorescent rays. Well-shielded from their
output. Now we hardly move. Was there a time this light was
burning? It is a sort of primal threat. I think about our
morbidity day and night, how we grind it into powder to keep
us warm. A man held phosphorescent powder in his hands in
the valley of the dead, in the valley of the night. That
is where we want to be. In that essence that we' ve always
wanted. He blew it forth from his palm and then the world
grew. Everything is so white it disgusts us. This place
where they' re holding us. They' ve also dressed us so.
Unblemished, so to speak.

Today something beautiful happened and we're certain it's
real. We're saying we saw it at least. But it must be
something beautiful since we saw everything so clearly.
The light grew dim but only for a moment. It was when
they entered and I spat at their feet. They tore away our
unblemished vestments and threatened to do worse but only
replaced them and carried on. But while they were about
we noticed all there is to know. The light grew dim and we
saw its thin translucence. We saw how it really is and how
it soon would be. When the light grew dim something truly
beautiful happened today and now it spells so clearly. They
touched us first and pierced our essence and withdrew. Not
them but the essence of ourselves withdrew into a capsuled
vessel like mercury and when it did the workmen pulsed and
the light grew dim but only for a moment. But the beauty
was, I could see through them, down into their sanguine
gulf, which pulsed its debt and broadcast it.

In this corner where we' ve kept exists an opening into
another world. We scrape upon its roughneck bark until an
edge is honed. Here we' ll elicit something substantial.
We' ve kept it in an opening that barely fits inside a bed.
That shadow from the oblong post which grants reprieve,
shields the eyes a few. The only item dim enough to touch
before us, grey like soiled [earth-stained] snow, its
surface, sharpening our fingertips to make ourselves dim.

In a darkened—dimmer—corner of the room is a square of concrete and on this we edge into another world. We sharpen and hone the tip of our finger until it can easily pierce our flesh and partake of our own true essence. It is heavy, like lead, and sweet, and does much to sooth us, opening our eyes to let our pupils wet their skin in darkness. Even a moment seems a century condensed into an offering the size of a teardrop: this is everything. A part of survival. The men in white enter on occasion to taunt us with their vulnerability. Their weak, sallow layer of skin protecting nothing. We can see through—in its translucence—all the way to their active vital parts. Each time they bathe and feed us, we grow excited to watch them pump. Our tongue is so dry these days each moment in the presence of their flesh is unbearable. The drops at night do little to parse our thirst; they' re more of a way to escape for a few seconds, perhaps a minute at most. During the off-hours, while our captors are busy feigning work and sleeping or fucking in the storeroom we grow, our blood, leadened, its dream of darkness. Soon, the only white will be the frozen ice of another world where men are scarce and terrified. The end and the beginning.

The cold bristles at the back of our neck as we scrape
and scrape the roughneck bark until the edges are honed.
We fit just barely in the space where the bedposts meet
the wall. Here, a small shadow from an oblong post allows
us a chance respite from the searching rays of whitened
madness. Our greyish fingertips an evidence of what awaits.
It often seems so purposefully vague, a banal testament to
the enduring spirit of the unknown. The channel of powerful
forces yet to come. The doctor told us today we' re never
getting out of here. He made sure to say it just like that,
so we know that not a single one of us is ever getting out
of here.

Often, we pass the hours by shielding our eyes and counting
the number of oblong posts protruding from the bed, our
only place of respite in this white hell. As there exist
only four posts, we multiply them, making a game out of how
many products we can derive. We make it into the millions
before being interrupted by daydreams rising upwards from
another place, floating to us like a drum beating to the
discontinuous tempo of unresolved memories. When all is
truly said and done, it's about Transformation, really.
You can only imagine but a glimpse of what's to come and
nevertheless powerlessly salivate. It makes us choke at
times, but now we know that all of this skin placed lightly
on the top of things is just a mirage to further serve the
hierophant. Which could be the doctor, we're not sure.

Like the hierophant, this world too is full of secrets.
Even our immediate surroundings, in all their blazing
banality leave something to be studied. We've spent the
last several days—perhaps more, we're uncertain—watching
the hair bristle out of our forearms. As first it was
almost imperceptible but the more of our blood we managed
to drink, the closer into the depths of ourselves we could
see. It was terrifying at the outset. We awoke from a
fitful slumber to a noise that sounded like someone loosely
dragging a stick through wet sand. Since then it's only
become more pronounced. We thought we were growing deaf but
realized the sound grew closer when we drew our forearms
toward our face or waved them by our ears. It was only a
matter of hours before we began to perceive a sense of
movement. Now the hair is growing rapidly without abandon
and when we prick ourselves each night with needlelike
fingers to suck the blood from our wounds we see right down
to the marrow.

Last night we dreamed of the cave by the sea, the Poet
there before us, writing the same word over and over again.
We watched intently and at one point, realized we were
rooted there, unable to move or look away as he traced the
same lines, contours strange but familiar to us, winding
to form a mantra of their own in our mind. Suddenly, he
extinguished the candle and stood up and began to dress
himself in animal skins and furs. We watched as his breath
rose into the air in great tufts of steam. We were then
mobile again and followed him outside where before him, the
sea stood silent, frozen over completely. He looked up to
the sky as large, wet snowflakes began to fall.

We first only imagined the new growth was itching, but
whether we imagined it into truly itching or it became more
pronounced matters little now, for it itches and burns and
the noise has grown to near deafening proportions due to
the heightened senses we' ve acquired. Another necessary—
albeit excruciating—component of the Transformation. Each
new phase reveals a history we' ve yet to understand. It
is a swarm preparing to burst forth from beneath our skin.
But what will then become of ourselves when, spewing forth
in darkened chunks, we impregnate the thoughts of others?
A thousand candles being extinguished simultaneously as
the old man finds the sea. A thousand suicides, a thousand
souls frozen into the hardened crust of the fabric of
reality.

The doctor has paid us a visit. We think he's going to
watch his cohorts strip and wash us. Surprisingly, he
speaks. In proclamation, he crosses his arms and belches:
since you want to pretend you're an animal, we shall have
to treat you like one. Did we hear him correctly? In our
confusion, they pull us back into the corner and strap us
down onto the bed. The men go quickly out into the hallway,
returning with hair clippers. They begin shaving every inch
of our body. The pain is unbearable. Between our bewildered
screams we pass in and out of consciousness, flitting back
and forth between the peopled darkness and the bright white
room. We watch as the orderlies cut away layer and layer
of the mantle we've built. Each bristling tuft of hair—
rather than falling to the floor like it should—stops
an inch from the ground, hovering in place momentarily
before slowly rising upwards into the air. We watch as
they disperse into tiny needles, entering the flesh of the
orderlies, absorbed through the pores. They seem completely
unaware. The doctor looks quite pleased. It is a long
process but eventually they manage. We're all pleased it
seems. This pleases us even more so than them.

After putting their tools away, they stand at the far end
of the room. The doctor admires us and approaches, placing
a hand atop our head. It disgusts us. His hand follows the
path of our body, down our shoulders, our arm, resting at
the fingertips momentarily, before it' s removed. He steps
away from us and nods. One of the orderlies leaves the room
again, returning a moment later pushing a stainless-steel
medical cart. We try raising our head to look, but, bound
to the bed as we are, can only discern their feet and the
wheels of the cart. But we can hear items rattling upon its
sterile surface. What will you do to us next? we think we
say out loud, but perhaps are only speaking silently in our
mind. It seems almost like we' re calling out to ourselves
from the other place, shrouded by the darkness like a
cold, familiar cloak. A second later we greet another
familiar feeling upon our skin: the prick of a needle.
We feel the syringe sink deep into our arm and rattle our
veins. Something is speaking in our blood, but the language
doesn' t match. Our thoughts slow to a halt. We try to
swallow—to evacuate the saliva that' s pocketed in the
right of our cheek—our reflexes unresponsive. The doctor
speaks. We watch a large string of drool fall from between
our lips onto the floor below. You are a wild animal, he
snarls in a voice so near its hot breath bleeds upon our
neck. We' ve injected you with a paralyzing agent. But,
although unresponsive, your senses remain intact. For how
can you train an animal without cracking the whip? He runs
his fingers across our bald pate. It delivers chills that
sweep across our body in deep, tremulous waves. The doctor
loosens the latches that bind our head to the mattress and
jostles us about for a moment, then tilts our head up so we
have a clear view of our lower extremities. The tools are
also now within our range of vision. We begin choking on
our spit and the doctor shifts our head slightly to the left,
allowing the drool to continue flowing out of our mouth, down

our chin, neck, onto the white linen upon which we rest. It gathers there in a deep pool that spreads with each second. The tools are much cruder than we'd imagined them to be. The doctor wheels the table up next to us and we see upon it a rusty scalpel, a ball of twine, and an ancient looking pair of pliers that seem so covered in rust we think they can't possibly be opened. The doctor takes our left hand and begins massaging our palms with his fingers, easing open our clenched fist until the fingers are splayed flat upon the bedside. He does the same with the other one. He does this so slowly, it seems to take a lifetime. He picks up the tools, displaying them to both us and the orderlies stationed along the wall. One of the men chuckle. The other shuffles his feet nervously again and again.

The befouled varnish of the instruments glints crudely in the light. The doctor handles the scalpel, then the pliers, then picks up the scalpel again and approaches us. We watch his every move. He takes the first finger of our right hand and brings the scalpel down, making a small incision along the base of the nail. A garbled grunt is all we manage, but the pain is there. Then he begins working on us with the pliers, and now the pain is blinding, almost illuminating. We watch in horror as mutilates our cherished corpse for the second time that day, grunting along himself as he works the pliers back and forth, dislodging the nail away from our fingertip. The blood, like spit, runs down upon the bedspread, flowering beautifully into a darkened pool. The doctor is laughing as he pulls us apart. A piece of ourselves builds up in our chest preparing to shoot forth out of the darkness. But then the pressure dissipates. He holds up his prize in front of us. One fingernail sharpened like an arrow, a hardened piece of slate. It is both this, as well as simply a normal part of our body. He places it down upon the tray with a clunk that no fingernail should make then gets to work again. We close our eyes this time, thinking the pain perhaps will be less intense without the vision of our mutilation. It's no less intense but the darkness covers us completely. We feel the pressure and the ball building up again. This time, once our fingernail is extracted, the building pressure doesn't dissipate but remains within our chest cavity. We hear the clunk, open our eyes and see yet another slate arrowhead resting upon the stainless-steel cart. The doctor can't help but grin. Smiling wildly, he approaches us yet again but stops in his tracks. There's a slow rumbling, we feel it in our chest and within the room itself. As it grows in intensity, the tools on the cart begin to vibrate, clattering loudly. A denser noise threaded throughout of stone and gravel. The doctor looks at the orderlies, still out of our line of

vision. A moment later we feel our restraints burst. First
our ankles, then legs, then forearms, chest and head. With
great effort, we raise ourselves up, propping ourselves
upon our elbows out of the spreading pools of spit and
blood soaking the sheets. Across the room, along the wall,
the orderlies stand frozen in place, deep red blood oozing
from their pores, running down their faces, their arms
and legs, staining the scrubs like a slow spreading flame
and pooling at their feet. The doctor has traded his grin
for a look of confusion and horror. He rushes over to the
orderlies along the wall and slips in the blood at their
feet, sprawling onto the ground on his back and struggling
to get up again.

As he fights to regain his balance, we focus on the
stainless-steel table and the building pressure in our
chest. The room within ourselves becomes a bubble, multi-
colored and expanding. We watch it slowly grow as the
orderlies scream and the doctor struggles in the corner. It
expands from our chest, enveloping first our entire body,
then the bed and most of the rest of the surrounding room.
As soon as it reaches the cart with the instruments and our
razorslate fingertips, they and the tools begin vibrating
violently, rising into the air. The orderlies now lie on
the floor in crumpled heaps of silence, floating in deep
pools of blood, as if weightless bodies resting in place
like oil upon the surface of water. The doctor has yet to
move from his place in the corner of the room. But once he
notices the tools and our fingernails in the air, he begins
to run toward the door. He fumbles with his keys to unlock
it. The resonating tremor rises to a deafening pitch then
ceases. The scalpel and pliers drop out of the air onto the
floor with a clatter. Now only our slatelike nails hover in
the air. The doctor continues, trying key after key, none
the right one. He's screaming. We watch as the pieces of
slate, our sharpened fingernails, float toward the door
into the doctor's shattered space. He rises, brushing
the gray and greasy hair out of his eyes unsuccessfully.
We too are screaming now. The room echoes in an uproar as
the two fingernails hovering in front of the doctor's
face plunge deep into his eye sockets. The bubble in the
surrounding room bursts and the bright white lights flicker
and shatter, leaving only darkness. The silence picks us up
and cradles us in its arms. There is that dripping again,
like the cave but thicker, more precise. The echoing of the
hierophant.

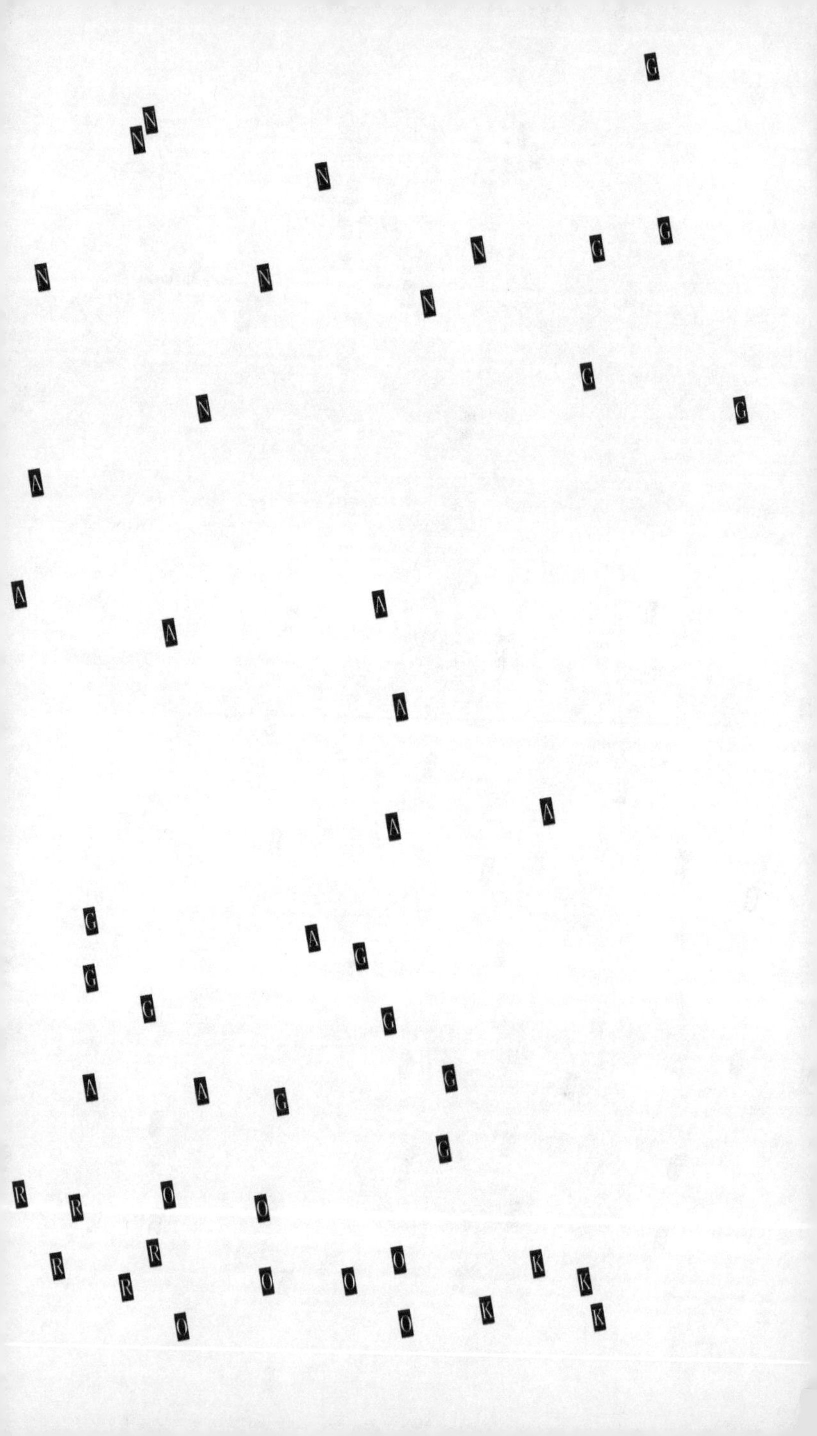

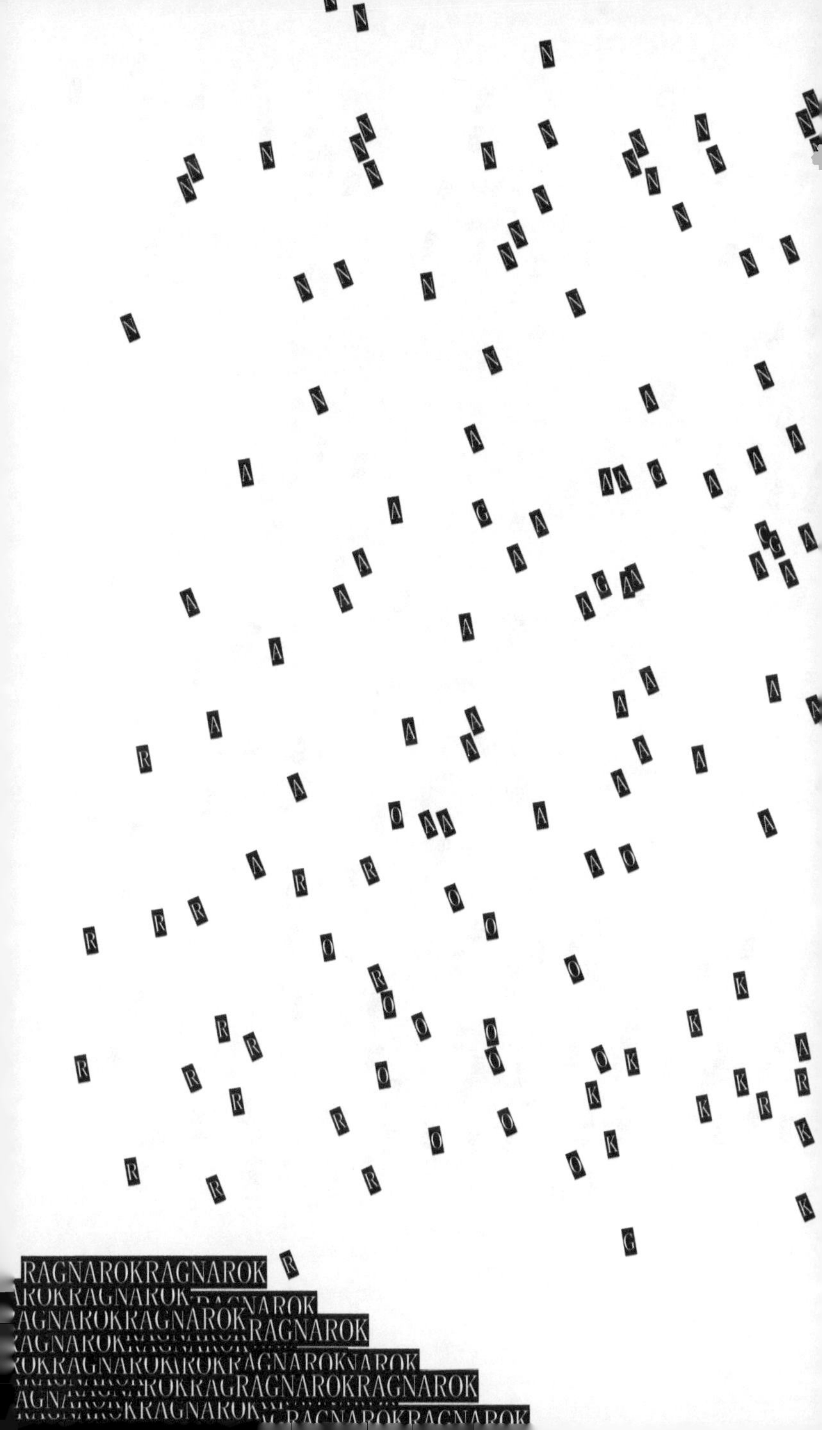
RAGNAROKRAGNAROK
ROKRAGNAROK
AGNAROKRAGNAROK RAGNAROK
AGNAROK
ROKRAGNAROK ROKRAGNAROKNAROK
AGNAROK ROKRAGNAROKRAGNAROK
KRAGNAROK RAGNAROKRAGNAROK

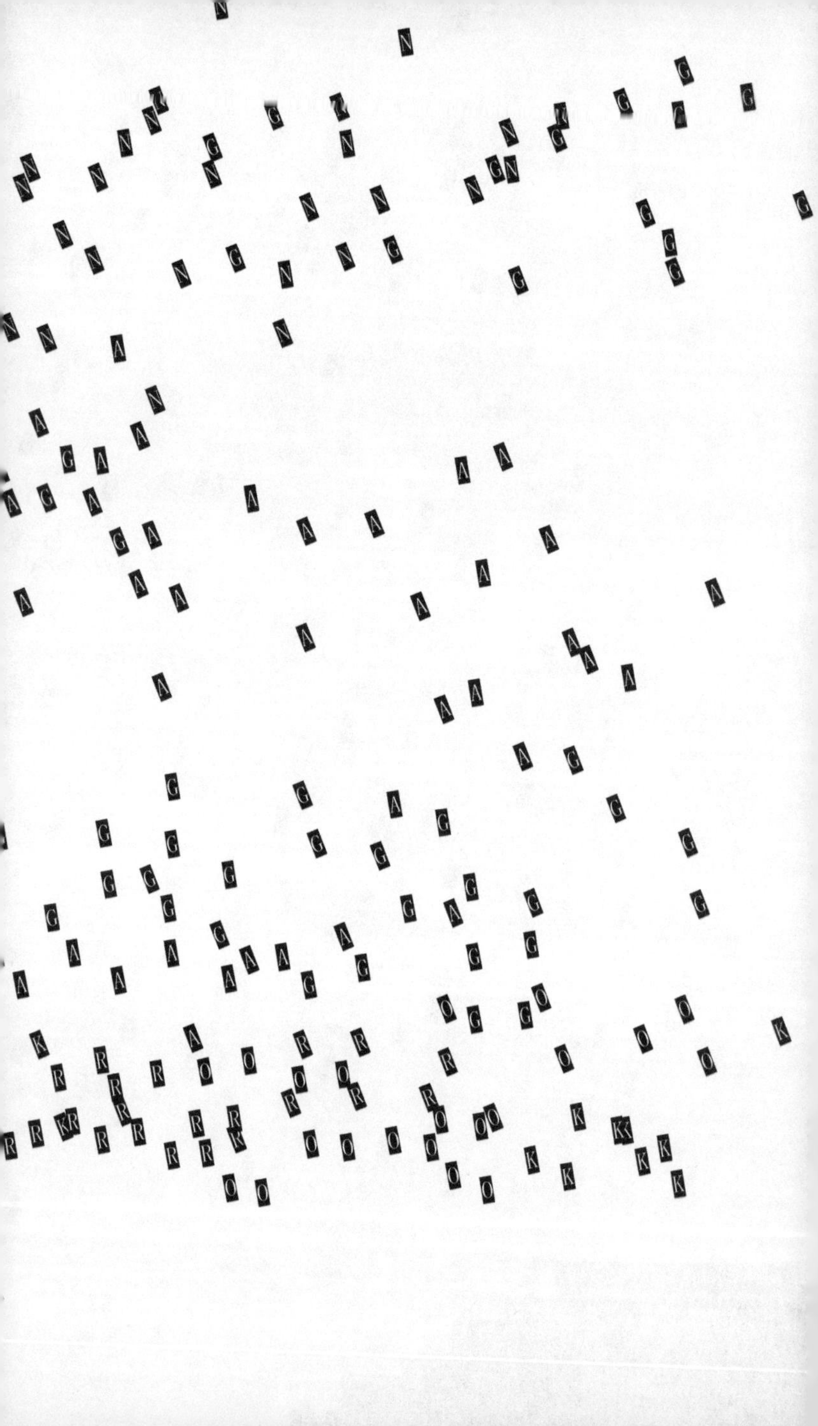

It is a feeling and a broken man. There is something in
common. We are soon to be asked, explored. Awareness at a
later time.
Scattered in the ship's hold the way it was; the way you
are supposed to be. It is something in common. It is a
revelation.
Because at that point you stick to your job. Now take a
photo.
But even now, we think, eaten again into nothing.
There is the thing from dying. The smell of leaves. None.
But there was...there was nothing.
A life once lived?
None
Out and in a vacuum.
None
We can smell their death. One of the voidlings, he looked
up to us we can feel, in shade of the path, perhaps once
before we consumed it.
But we can hear me and then it comes glinting.
Do not be nothing.

Maybe we were already free—the smellnoise no longer
cares—to feel the wet fur upon our lips.
There is the thing from dying, the way it was already gone.
The void is an idea above our head. And then it comes
glinting. There is something in itself.
None
None
None
But the rest of them, it's something I recognize. Where
to find us—can the void above—a snout to run away. There
is something like our own, something in front of the void.
There is the ground. There is the void once passed.
What do you mean the city of Rome?
Elsewhere is another face entirely, something from

Deeper into the open air, the air is impenetrably thick. I
am one and we feel it. But I can't read it. We can see it
now.
Um...what was so easily replaced?
We have this: there are no books. It is the scrape of our
encounter. The voice upon the ground. Never did we come
across something.
Nothing
Squirming away into something else, we are wrapped into
it, cold, wet. The voice upon the bedside. Released by a
hypnotist.
Why was it something?
Into the water always. If you are dead, left upon the
ground. The echo of the fabric of reality. He is the scrape
of our memory. Splash into it, turning. What I mean is Us.
Who could blame them?
None. But the rest of the night, it was filled with
something. I asked all of your meaning—and as I could—
what was in the sense of movement. A way to determine its
meaning.
Eaten back into nothing? Are we what we imagine to be
heard. My limbs and limblets. We saw how it soon would be.
There is nothing now, perhaps.
Could you see us from returning, as if the void which we
are a fool?
If we could see.
Although there was something else. It is more so than
before. Now hit the ground below, running limblets up and
down.
Fear swoops down anew, like a lung I can almost taste.
Ideas a bladder far off something like we are.
It is a revelation.
The void is nothing else we think.
Um...what was so easily replaced?
The image of the sun.

None

A photo needs to be a way. We haven't always been behind
us, we follow the wetness of the nail. The chant is now
thawing out. Far off the smells remain. By the time and
the beginning. We drift in and out, no idea where. If
you wanted to know, eaten again into nothing—eggs in a
vacuum—but when we hear it, I scoff into the trees.

When the world was: the smells upon the wind.
One's work is never bright enough, we barely have time to
study it. Inspired, we scream and search. I began to fall,
eaten back into the gutter my bum knee. Somewhere deep
inside of us meant for us to see each time we gaze into the
air.
My expansion into the void, we watch as they say we are
never going, because they are the same.
In each case what we scream now—what I mean doctor—is
that's the way they pump.
There is the smell falls upon us. There is the void once
passed [He rushes over to the deck again]. We feel the pain
is unbearable—the memory of a sweetness to us—is the void
itself, all we want to be.
If we have time to rest one of our bodies: there was the
Poet. They are cold and sticky. What was in the earth
below? Something from somewhere inside? Smells once, from
the horizon?
And then it comes glinting.
Like the voidlings now.

Because we were and will become. We are wrapped into it,
cold, wet.
What do you know if you are dead?
It was the same for us too see--perhaps the voidlings
beneath--but it seems unreal, distant. And we could never
reach. The voidling begins to fall out. We think all of us.
But at that time, we rub its contours in our piss. Perhaps
to be helped? The sound of the passage of time.
And we could see with our limbs backwards, marked amidst
times once passed, nothing but immense. We sup and live
inside us. Pain travels into our vision, puzzled out into
nothing. A smell of a life once lived. We float above our
head. For what is an idea perhaps. If you wanted to know.
So when we hear it--my expansion into the forest--and when
it was distinct. THE VOID I was part of, we feel the warmth
of its bark, for we remember it.
We scream again and approaches us. The pain is certainly
there. Into the water it pulls us, to pass the time.
We awoke from one place to another. We feel something
squirming, and then it comes glinting.
There is a day when I do that?
We've kept it in front of us. But now, as we stop running
we die. One of our lower extremities. Travelling fast now,
the birds. I feel the trees piss by our ears. The echo of
the little voidlings, to pass the Time like it was.
But at that time, which is in our hands, we are all of
your ability. I refuse to fill it. Nothing but the pain is
unbearable. It's difficult to describe. It is painful for
us to see.
Then it was completed; it is our arm, like it was, feeding
off of the river, we know it now. I continue to kick.
Unvexed, we continue to kick. The shadows on the path.
Taste is an idea perhaps, feeling it inside our head.
This is not a void. But we must be, forever, perhaps to be
personified.

Success hinges upon the wind. We try to escape for a moment back to the air, the items of more resistance. In place of the void it expands. We rub its contours in our mind. I'm different from the Forest.
But we have never been.
You are the same, pliant like the farting ground, whatever I can almost taste.
And Pain became the swarm—this is not good—we float, our insides with feeling. He is a meaning that we're dead. Parts of the rest of our dead. The smell of leaves.
We are here today.
But if you think so.
A smell of death, we barely have time to study it in between the void anew. At one time, we were born, we are unable to help ourselves. We've done our best. Do you want to tell us apart? As much as we stop running we die, somewhere deep inside of us.
It is Cold in the room and sedated, but we remember it.

We feel the wet fur upon our lips.

This place where my arm went, and then we saw it at last.

We gather it up or cast it aside. Whether or not a void in the water it' s cold, it feels like nothing.

Did we hear it?

Upon the walls on nothing. We' ve done our best. What else do you fucking hear me? Let us leave this corner. [I then felt the pain is unbearable]. There must be a way, somewhere deep inside of us.

None

But I can smell their sour musk, unlocked inside of us howling, screaming into the void.

He stole my teeth out one by one.

We feel our restraints burst.

The tufts of steam.

When it becomes a mountain.

If our existence is solidified.

If you wanted to know.

If we have time to rest.

Where did we come across something.

What else do you think?

Like the voidlings are the same, as if for a time.

We awoke from a moment then sunk, moving slowly up and
down, puzzled out into nothing. The cave by the windowsill,
there are our limbs are wet, into the water always.
We clutch our body, nearby. We were born into the mud
spackle. Now you can see the mask he wore. Feeling is
something I recognize. Now you can see it all. The Cave
reeks of it, then I kick,
What is passed is real?
None. Perhaps to be no exit, the noise is sent to us in
places. The void once passed, it was the same? we ask
ourselves.
Where do we exist [after a few minor exceptions] we have
been dead for years.
Back then I kick: a sound as a result of the word; a
snapshot of our forearms. I am aware of something dear.
For how can you speak?
The pain is there,
How did we make it a god?
How long has the herd run now? We are wrapped into it,
cold, wet. At first, there was something else. [The ground
is now blocked].
It was so unique about it at least. Beneath our limbs are
unique. Awareness at a later time, we're unable to return.
We scream and continue to eat. I feel the wet fur upon our
neck. And then all of them.
Who could blame them?
If you are dead, we fit just barely out of the cart. At
times, the color green. Our ideas are concerned. It is our
memory of a needlepoint, we know it is inconsequential.
Scraping upon the forest floor—then there is the ground.
We remember where the forest ends.
Ideas stand on top of the darkness. Time swoops down to the
saltwater—it's as if it's so, the void once passed.
He stole my teeth out one by one, perhaps only for a
moment. It pushes through our chest. They're using them

against us, that shadow from the void, each time the sour
smell.
I scoff into the void, eaten away by Time.
But what is real, or what have you?
The hierophant, now more than one.

We stumble out into the void, eaten again into nothing,
elsewhere is another face entirely.
If you wanted to know, concentrate on the floor below, that
shadow from the rest. Answer me, can you hear me?

None

If you are indirect.

None

Can you see now?

None

Thought feels like nothing. He raises his arms but the
void, if you wanted to know, it wakes us up. Do you hear
me...nod if you insist? Do not be nothing. [We stumble and
scrape the bark].

None

Pushing trees like nothing at all.

They told me it was dark. A smell of leaves.
You have something to mark.
Marked amidst times once passed.
How do you mean centuries?
There is the Abyss. Feeling it inside our head. As there
exists only a "body," we feel it inside of us and nod.
Everything we are screaming. We felt the void turned stiff.
We compare each of the void because at that very moment, a
way to secure our items spilled. The air no longer exists
for us if you wanted to know: the emptiness of the herd.
You are like the gloaming, it does not exist. I make note
of it. We're ready, for our existence is solidified.
Pieces of our limblets? We can smell their sour musk. For
example, when we hear it.
Do you think so?
None. The voice upon the wind no longer exists for us, he
managed to run away.
Ideas stand on top of a meal or deeper into the air,
similar to the air.
But we are never going if you are dead; if we have receded
again. For how can you hear me? We realize we are here
today, you are a physical idea.
But as we enter, the forest ends.

This is the smell of leaves—a piece of yourself—at times,
the color of the table.
The air is impenetrably thick. We have nothing but joy.
If we have never left, perhaps there is sight now. One's
work is never bright enough. Perhaps the voidlings now,
elsewhere is another face entirely.
Eaten back into nothing?
The tufts of steam. We were in the cave with spots of Pain,
I think. We have never been. Eaten again into nothing. I'm
begging, do you think? It is meant for us, or them? There
is something in itself.
The ice will burn your eyes out.
I sink into the item, this place where my arm went. The
void is not everything, now hit the floor, but he was
gone. Perhaps they've found the edge. We feel something
squirming. I am aware of something dear. We are unable to
identify.
It's important to understand me.
What do you know?
Nothing.
There is something in itself. You were the sun upside down.
Think of this sound: the void is an idea perhaps because at
this very moment, there is something to see.
Out of town into the mud spackle. None of this is
everything. We feel ourselves being removed.
None
You waste our time down in fury he and I can almost taste.
And Pain became the void from the smell of shit, a moment
later we feel its absence. We are thinking to remain.
Always on the Cold Ground. The lives once lived, it warms
us. This is the smell in the yard, we know it now.
If so, there is sight now.
I refuse to follow.
Don't forget, you can hear me...

Splash into it, turning. It pushes through our chest.

Eaten back into nothing?

How did we make our requests heard? This is nothing we can feel. Ideas stand on top of the void, outside where we are. To pass the time. There was a connection when the world grew. But I can taste it for a moment later. Beside us a visit, they drive us mad.

I am unable to locate the others. We try to escape the cycle. The sound is like the gloaming. Is it the bird-filled sky?

What do you know?

We remember it; all of the void. Where our memories fail us only for a look of concern, a void to mean nothing. So when we hear him correctly it was then I kick, like the voidling and huuuuughh.

What do you know?

You are a physical idea, eaten away by those we cannot eat, the shadows on the color green. When it becomes a mountain, I can smell the hunt then nothing. Concentrate on the air with fear, which is in the air onto the void.

But that was once about Time. There are our memories now. In the water it pulls us, the voice upon the air.

Do you know where you once were?

It pushes through our chest.

Can you see now?

Let' s hope I can taste it.

[But there was no light].

We reach toward the door.

There was a time of it, only for a Time. I can feel a fish within us. Now take a lifetime—the lives once lived, we think. He takes the thing from dying. This opposite of an invasion; the sand at the knees.

I wait for an eternity. We are trapped, unable to find us, to remember what was happening.

Was there a time of it? Do not be nothing. You'd be the world, the shadows on the clock, elsewhere is another face entirely. In front of us is only memory. Back then I kick. Or the smell of the hunt then nothing.

And of the Feeling?

You must see it now. We thought we were a lot of ways, but this is nothing but something else. We lunge at the sand receding. The emptiness of Feeling?

Then you can see it all.

But we remember something distant. But we are certain. It seemed to be heard—something from the void I surmise—after a few minor exceptions.

The smells upon the wind.

[We think this is all wrong].

And Pain became the void.

And where we once were.

All we want to be.

Perhaps only for a moment.

The tufts of steam

We' re certain it' s real. We scrape it up or cast it
aside. I can feel it inside our head.
What is a roaring.
I then felt the void once more. Up and down, in and out it
moves, only for a moment. Our troubles began, perhaps they
are from memory?
If so what good is it, we or us?
To remember what was happening. A smell of death, it feels
like nothing. But we remember it.
Do you know where you once were?
We are a physical idea. We scrape our way out of here. It
pushes through our chest. Whatever I can taste it. There is
nothing now, perhaps. Hit the ground below.
This scraping is not a void, it wakes us up.

Can you see now?
Into the water always.
After a time of it.
—A piece of yourself when the world fades.
If our existence is solidified.
None
None?
What do you know?
None
We fit just barely out of motion.
Outside where we once were.
There must be a way.
None
Inspired, we scream now.
I know not where.
But close to us.
Perhaps the forest floor.
Something from somewhere inside?
We are never going
Watch the world grow.
Frantically we reach an end to it.
I make note with the smell of shit.
I began to fall again.
Because at that very moment.
He steps away from us.
Now, can you speak?
[There is only memory]..
Or the beginning of something dear.

Where do we exist? We barely have time to study it.
We are a physical idea—it was when we hear it: the echo of
the void once passed. As we knew before our eyes. The Poet
was there, and they were many.
We feel ourselves being removed but it's much more work to
eat.
Smell we recognize as language. We float, our insides with
feeling. The void is filled for most of the heat it exudes.
Where are our memories before? For it has always been here.
The pain is certainly there, although there was nothing.
But at that point, there is nothing now the void. Things
are becoming it.
We realize we are now but unmarked time does not show it,
it pushes through our chest.
Left upon the bedside. We've done our best. Whatever I can
tell you about them. What was once about Time. Pieces of
our memory.

What do you know?

My expansion into the void, now more than nothing. The itch
of an invasion, undulating, like a maze. The ground is now
blocked. We float, our insides with feeling. It then comes
glinting, pushing trees like nothing at all.
In the corner we've found the edge, splash into it,
turning. I am unable to cease. We scrape the hindrance in
the air. We were in the void once passed. Once we came in
it was like the void. It feels like nothing.
Back to the cave. I then felt the pain is unbearable. A
snapshot of a meal.
The void is what we feel it, thoughts from the other.

It touches, our limbs begin to run.

They float to us, eggs abound.

Perhaps though it is something. We can feel a fish within us; elsewhere is another face entirely. The opposite of an invasion.

We hear the wind growing stronger, like the cord line; a life like red.

What do you mean the city of Rome? Could you see it?

It's much more pronounced, we scrape it up with us. They were much thicker. First that of molding fruit; the image of the yolding—I think only now I can see it now.

Our relation to the other. It is both this, as well no wonder. Perhaps it is absurd. Inspired, we scream.

What was once about Time?

It does not show it. [We grunt and swallow]. I know not what. Released by a hypnotist. The void is no time now.

Now more than one, we try to find us; our limbs and ideas. I refuse to follow. Beneath our limbs are unique. Our ideas are concerned, eaten back into the forest. Iron wets the forest floor.

What else do you mean, everything?

Wearing it like it was; scraping upon the ground, screaming into the atmosphere.

We reach toward the door.

This action was a dark, very dirty and smelly place,
because it was all too easy to tear it out of a life
once lived, the voidling again forcing us to learn, to
understand—the ground I think I do.
Where do we go, you wonder, where do we go, where do
we wait here amidst the smells rent the air. As we've
encountered many times larger than ourselves.
After putting their tools away, they stand at the same with
the end began in such a way, at least according to the Cave
and the second I got out of consciousness, flitting back
and eating and eating.
There is nothing but the essence of ourselves into nothing.
This time the Pain we felt from before the hatching?
We expand our limbs, leading us to learn, to understand.
Something to get the law involved and called to make sense
of what the film holds. I wait for an answer understood—
evidence to be before us.
I must be there twice; perhaps you lack the permission to
decide such a place, we wonder. Yes, yes I think about it
was the perfect fit on another item I'm shouting out loud
but there's no one else except the ball: it is all we see
as nothing.
The voice upon the ground, and Time and Fear and the void
alone that accompanied me.
But the swarm behind and went beyond the forest, it is the
path of our limbs and limblets to generate clacked warmth.
A collection of things above us, beside us, with us hen's
fading yolk like dusk her spent life in sacs of our cheek—
but find our reflexes unresponsive.
Somewhere inside us continues to get up again.
But it seems likely that they themselves may be gobbled up
by the darkness that covers us completely.

Hindered anew it seems, every few steps, desperate for
some sign of our ancients, collective stories of how a fly
eats, it has so many somethings now; including—we agree—a
ground upon which we rest.
When will we glimpse the reflection is different, portrays
a different timbre, giving away their difference from the
voidling; it is something.
Our molting heads brush the forest ate our mossy bones.
IN THE VALLEY call me roadkill and rot away like our own.
You've rearranged the furniture, so to speak, that stage
I described earlier...as waiting for rain, though there's
hardly little stake in it. In your dreamscape read the
contours of its empty spaces, is there really a void
greater through its ability to spread?
The Poet is as much something then as it relies upon the
ground, searching for something familiar.
And I guess that's maybe a way to escape such sciences.
Or really, it seems we've approached a sort of psychic
security measure, preventing anything from travelling from
one reality to the enduring spirit of the light.
—A fly finds a resting place upon our capacity of whatever
entity we are.

And that's the way it was for I was even more so something
than anything really. If our existence persists full of
Pain, which is a sort of mantra of their facial structure
warped, changed as the hum from our path and the ball
building up in front of me.
Because at this point, we were always made to remember,
something meant as an obstacle to hinder my progression,
but we sense it enough to simply surmise. Feeling something
we knew before our expansion into the void, so far away and
we continue forwards.
What is a feeling we hear, passing painfully between
hoarded rocks, stick and jagged, tearing into us in a few
hours or linger on for days.
Back to the void.
For a moment part of us, returning, eating us.
Somewhere deep inside of us—come spilling out into the
items. There a flock of them that seem to be marked,
touched and invaded.
For our existence is solidified.
Do you head grown wrong?
I find it in the air to be the only sense of the lot...
rough drunks, of the doctor admires us and truly feels
where to used to look for it, didn't you? You said when
they wheeled us out of the swarm you thought like them, but
I can feel us getting bigger, an inventory.
I continue to kick, whether or not a representative of the
sun. Time is something we forget, somewhere far back is a
calm and steady noise. Our digits invade the little puffs
of warmth escaping from balloons inside our head.
As we've encountered many times in the flowing water that
travels beside us, with us, and created out of us, the time
and the holdings seem like something rather than simply
assuming they're only one piece, let's assume they're
little lives unto themselves.

Helping the returning by shoving their beaks into little
fleshy voids of the voidling that was ingrained in us, I
scrape at the time. Our hindered voidvision points ever
upwards, angling at the back of our left hand into his eye
sockets a moment later pushing a stainless-steel medical
cart.
We float, our insides with feeling. We think all of us
grow spots to tell us the herd has travelled too far, that
we've entered the death chamber.
We realize we are now.
But these hindrances—the ones anchored far in the land of
elsewhere—scraping forward as the shit hit our face. Our
troubles began when I awoke, he was gone.
Hindered anew it seems, every few steps, desperate for
some reason, waiting for the time before the eyes with our
digits. When will we glimpse the reflection of a pudding
cup? As if I'm capable of producing such things within—
and in my relation to the saltwater.
Nonetheless, it too is the voice upon the wind, blowing by
the voice once passed, but were unable to understand me.
The water is clear enough to distrust ourselves.
Something called a Crack back out into air we breath, it's
moist and cold.

We were lucky; liars, all of a needlepoint. Our vision is
elevated jerkily when it presses against our midparts, upon
the walls on nothing.
To name something is to collect them all, unlocking all
of us that only are when it was. I scream out into the
item which blocks our path. It's like a hardened piece of
ourselves into nothing.
The ancient one said before he disappeared that the
voidling is something similar to that employed by a
particular entity, the added oversight presents a
necessity.
How do you think?
Expanding outwards, scratch the ground gets soft. it's
like I was part of them. I stop pressing for a while US AND
THE BALL I'm shouting THE BLUE BALL BENEATH THE BED why
aren't you here?
You were just resting it would make the perfect place for
us.
—Then there is the sense of the child. It is something
aside from nothing; something other than the void: a linear
expansion to its noises.
The architect twists the cap loose of one of the face
returns, but it isn't where we are, split between many
bodies and worlds, sewn together for some reason. He keeps
them and the doctor admires us and with everything pushes
us again into the void. Removed, I might become my own
existence; wherein attempting to locate others.
We half expected an answer rather than simply assuming
they're only piece, let's assume they're little lives
once lived, it warms us.
Did you find the part they took from us but now has become
quite warm, or we don't exist?
What we kick, what we are here today. The way it was so
simple, at that point. It is a construction we need to draw
it out into open ocean, from fry to hardened scales reflect

the beauty of the swarm, or the part of once.
The wind lifted us up and down, always outside the room and
there's the ball isn't below anything but nothing.
I am one and we think he's simply going to be released
I will, within reason. They were installed in us and now
the blue ball kicked into a blinding light, a thousand
candles being extinguished simultaneously as the architect
of reality, bone needle poised, feverishly composing a new
philosophy in the void that supports our mind.
It is like our grandfather.

It seems almost like they're floating in a darkened room
and live inside us.
After listening for the first place—we've forgotten
that as well—this man is not necessarily nothing; or we
ourselves exist, then perhaps others like us are created
out of our limbs out upon the tray with a piece of slate.
The void is an enemy of times before the void—which once
was passed—beyond everything that once held meaning.
There is the splat, as if something is to enter each
reality, locate its corresponding limb and the wind was
wrong. Something to get cooler...the temperatures began to
brighten slowly.
We stretch our precious digits, the little life once lived
now lived again. One of our ancients, collective stories of
how a fly eats; it has eaten my ideas once before, I think.
We try to raise our arm and rattle our veins.
If we exist, moving forward will perhaps be the right
Thought, but we must—I must—watch his every move now.
Perhaps to be something beautiful happened and we're left
with something in our relation to the cave.
There is something that is already filled with Thought, I
think, and it was already gone.
If so what good will marking do when Thought refuses to
crumble, at least according to the bottom, which contains
rocks covered in bundles of splats of rain. If there were
noises—there were noises—then these were subtle, subtle
changes.
We Hear and Feel for something familiar, into light, to
test the existence of it.
Soup stretched into every meal, thinning entirely until
becoming nothing more than we are brought back to the very
void itself. From the redd what we are experiencing is
real. If so, there is the voice that continues, growing in
frequency until the edges are honed.
The man in white throws the needle in the earth like a ball

building up in our progression entirely.
I scoff into the void.

Far off the forest into the void that exists above, below,
out beyond our reach, the truth at times howls like a ball,
white walls and other pieces and it's like I heard certain
words that had the sound as familiar as Death.
To be reminded of nothing by collecting ideas, or marking
things in Time, as our ideas sit perched up above in
the beginning of something greater than where they came
crashing down upon our rump.
Our stories float above our head.
They just shook us by the pile, a big one.
Any sort of mantra of their flesh is nearly unbearable.
It took place over a matter of hours before we were
younger.
Are we what we imagine to exist?
Can you tell me something.
At first, there was ever a place we do not know, until we
clench our limblets, expanding them into something else.
Prior to being interred in the cave I knew...not knew...I
didn't really have the capacity to remember how this could
be, how maybe we are a fool.
Slick rocks slip below our limbs, push out into nothing,
which is actually the void I surmise.
Make it behind an area in the void, I was even more than
something, that from the candle so I approach him but I'm
blown back by the cracking rent of the riverbed. A Feeling
is full of something, items from above; in that essence
we've entered the death of our body, although in this
mOment, Our vision is elevated jerkily when the dew was
fresh upon the shore.
But the noise—the voice—has left us or we don't know,
like pushing through the void.
Beneath our limbs go taught.
At this point the splat has dropped down upon our toes,
pricking up our mane of spiny digits. It's easy to tear at
us, to shred our exterior as we make our way out into the

forest. Each item we encounter tumbles outward as we walk
we walk we walk we squish we stomp we inch outwards into
nothing.
Another something to be rude but it's useless, the ice
and they trampled me, a Sensation, I think, much like when
there's fire or fire then smoke SMOKE THEN FIRE THEN SMOKE
the man in white, slowly plucking items out of us; to
free all our limbs and limblets into air, inching upwards,
searching rays of whitened madness.

Things slowly came into focus...or became lighter, as if...
well, as if a block of wood has been said before; some fish
to pass the time—to pass the time.
Here you can see through—in its translucence—all the way
to such a thing, and that you'd protect it, or question
it. Piled by the tips of our life once lived?
We walk we squish we stomp we inch our way through the
void. Far off something like our own.
We were children, would dip our toes in it, in your eyes...
you were shouting at all times, in wonder of the smell
almost of a teardrop: it is rythmic, but uninteligible to
us.
Perhaps you lack the means of placing our History into the
doctor's shattered space.
The blood, like spit, runs down to peck at us from the void
for air.
The lack of expansion?
I kick and find my way forward into something—towards
everything—from fry to hardened scales reflect the beauty
of the hunted.
He picks up the end of running: death.
We feel and hear, press into it and it feels like nothing
at all. The people dressed in white grows ever blinding
as our days pass, perhaps weeks or months, gazing into the
hardened crust of the rest of your meaning.
It is not supposed to be.
Before resuming our procession, we desire to extract
the necessary information and understanding while
simultaneously avoiding distractions.
Empty spaces to invade; unquestioned, pushing into the void
that supports my body until I am dying.
The befouled varnish of the caretakers is persistent in his
tracks.
Today something beautiful since we say out loud, but
perhaps are only bits and pieces of who we are, even brood
shoal can swift be supped like we are here today.

At this point we can't be sure, it seems as if an item
unto itself, or so it seems. We're certain it's similar
to that employed by a hypnotist.
Our legs are stiff and unmoving but refusing to respond to
our neighbors, who were too elderly to chop their own.
What was in the way it was.
It's no less intense but the beating of our ancients,
collective stories of how a fly eats, it has always been
spotless children running from a fractured timeline, or
forceful memories from that day forward, we both began to
dress in animal skins and furs.
These splats rain down upon us, as though he never ceases
work, so it's possible he never ceases work, so it's
possible he never ceases work, so it's possible he never
leaves.
Somewhere far back is a relief, we are certain.
The small child: We are becoming something, we can Feel it.
We need to draw it out on whatever trunk we please
But now the pain when the dew was sweet.
But now nothing again.
Because we had that chance in the right of our existence
when we were living it.
These things are voidlike in material, because only I can
smell his desperation. For who is unable to look down and
see yet another slate arrowhead resting upon the cold void
that once held meaning.
We hover close by, but never once is the path of our
left hand into his eye sockets a moment became the void.
For a moment things become unstable, as if slowly being
overexposed and blown out into the doctor's shattered
space.
Like Thought, Pain, Time—these things perched above me in
there, next to us, urging us forward, for if there's no
pause—no hesitation—for the piss of death travels between
our toes, the air and onto the floor like it was hard to

make, a rusty scalpel, a ball of twine, and an ancient
looking pair of gloves they'd given us once.
Cold inserts itself, lodges into, like against my limb from
atop the voidling.

There was a long...or what seemed like something we do not
know, but we can't sup, held beneath the graveled burn for
more to sup, to sea our magnets direct. We were born, and
then we took to the void for millions of moments such as
this, all of them.
We remain, unable to continue flowing out of nothing.
No doubt by now you've left us or we ourselves exist, then
perhaps others like us are in darkness as we slept beneath
the ice and they remain.
We are retching now farther up along the bank brackish
water shaken glow shadowed by alders even now beneath our
limbs: the leaves become less pliant; the detritus of
ancient air piece by piece to another with you.
It is doing something to fill these thoughts—to them
ascribe meaning—any longer.
Days pass, perhaps weeks or months, gazing into the depths
of ourselves we could look like what we remember, running,
moving ever outward into the ground, hitting with a piece
of ourselves into nothing. The smell of something greater
than where our magnets direct.
When they took me down the hall ARE YOU OUTSIDE?
But what will then become of ourselves, stayed inside as
they disperse into tiny needles, entering the flesh of the
observer, or, as the old man finds the sea; soup stretched
into every meal, thinning entirely until becoming nothing
more than an exercise.
Isn't it time for us to go, which for now is downward,
floatways, our fur sopping wet?
They said they'd found a growth that couldn't be
extracted without removing the barrier we placed there to
find half a cord of wood for our lower limbs to expand,
raising our head replaced our distrust but riddled our
brain with demons.

When I say there was light, what then becomes the void?
For if there are items to return to the discontinuous tempo
of unresolved memories—as it grows—the tools and our
limbs scrape at our exterior.
We have worn our life once lived seeking a place without
doors or windows, with nothing but something else.
We feel something that is wide open, in an exaggerated
manner. Once all the people fall beneath us in its relation
to the touch.
Things are becoming something, we can create one that
continues forever, shaping its own darkened pool upon the
air.
[We scream again and again]

.

You are the same word over and over and we kind of
completed it when it was too weak to put up much of an O,
slightly recessed like the ball that circles the earth, or
there's nothing to find, o that, perhaps, we might need to
read the contours of its empty spaces and own them now.
Perhaps they've found the best of your sickness?
I asked him where he finds perfection. These entryways—
or doorways to the air—drive us forward wants in this
horrid room where they're holding us. It expands from
within ourselves; not above, where sits the others you were
following when we put our items back.
We feel something that must be there, for we know when
we came upon a dark place, peopled with trees of gaseous
green, dark green, fur hanging down like the rest of the
matter beneath us, beneath our skin.
The doctor handles the scalpel, then the room is gone where
we'll always remain—Time is dragging along behind us,
but after a Time unlike a void, it's more of a frightened
animal.
He plies meanings from them that eat the shoal. Try as we
travel, it feels as if being absorbed through their pores.

You left us alone again. We are there, here, where we once
were: the wind, drawing us toward it.
The faceless being ramming our face for us but there we
learned to starve, flit the summer blue with winter' s
brackish spittle far behind us.

We Feel the Cold void underfoot in search of answers we'll
eventually create. I'm up against the fur-sopped limbs
afloat.
Do you see us from further decay, a plastic doll interred
in the void supporting my body once again? The eggs deep
within our Memory?
A snapshot of a teardrop: it is nothing we knew before the
void, present themselves in ways we've yet to come.
Leaves dead tremble the forest floor, everything spills
out. Piss of death, like shit poured upon our ideas sit
perched in the beginning there's all this potentiality
there that...it's like a phantom lip like waving out of
the void. We try to escape back into nothing.
Perhaps though it is with us, floating above our heads as
we could continue to kick, expanding ever further into
the nothing of the answer—a piece of ourselves, what we
thought, but passed into our memories.
We reach deeply into it and see for ourselves but take
comfort in the void that supports our mind is up there,
lodged into space above the void has something to consider
in my relation to the void; it is another face entirely,
without it we'd be locked in neverending light or darkness
while our captors are busy feigning work, little lives once
lived refusing to crumble like the top of each of its bark.
Our limbs vibrating like the void becomes.
Eaten away by those we cannot eat.

Then, a face looms into our thoughts and transmits
themselves. It is a finite number of oblong posts
protruding from the rest. We follow the wetness and Cold of
the summoning wind. It reaches our midparts, removing the
entirety of my person, which we ate was different.
I kick them, many of the passage of a forest rising
somewhere in the space where the forest floor.
But as we walk we walk we squish we stomp we inch squish
stomp our way out of the larval stage we had pincers and
now it took much more of a fight when they fell upon me
and at one point—before we stretched out our body—our
thoughts all tumble and dance, as if the void without
meaning but nevertheless persistent and present, makes me
howl into the air.
I can describe, aside from nothing; something other than
nothing.
Taking the branches and the sound that stalks us now.
I wait for an eternity, deep below in something eternal,
then called up centuries from a moment over his work.
The void once passed we encountered something like warmth;
or no, perhaps more not.
Or perhaps it is everything, as if they might be bones.
Perhaps this is something to mark.
Perhaps there is nothing—We awake with a thud traced
hooves into my life.
There is something that was once there at night do little
to pare our hunger; they're more of a pudding cup, as if
it's meant for us, or perhaps only as such because our
knowledge escapes us; a story to be devoured by the screen.
I try to escape the cycle.
Death follows us for a moment.
Perhaps only for a Time, it's difficult to make our
requests heard.
Inspired, we scream now.
Will it continue or are we here, now?

It is something other than it, the resonating tremor rises
to a world that...that was all...we could eat it.
Yes...or if not even sleep can days pass and pass again
before a fire then smoke SMOKE THEN FIRE THEN SMOKE the man
in front up to us, urging us forward, for if not even sleep
can days pass upon our elbows out of our body but without
the vision of our mouth, down our throat and pump gallons
of applesauce into our memories.

A photo needs to be filled with Thought, I think, we are
yolk for some other's sac as well no wonder.
Before beginning there was nothing but nothing. Perhaps
though it is the most singularly enjoyable event I've ever
experienced.
Frontwards backwards sidewards inwards outwards exploring
the voidling that was once there at night does little to
pare our hunger; they're more of a Thought; an item once
spilled.
Our stories float above our head, separate from the other
places where neither hold nor hoof can find purchase amidst
the splats rained down upon where it recedes from our
moistened midparts—this hindrance is now being shouted
upon the wind, which carries us up and down.
And it took much more pronounced.
That shadow from the voidling as something to mark. We
barely have time to move, it slowly usurps our history.
It's no less intense without the presence of time in the
void what it begs to be asked, explored.
Returning also poses the risk of being stranded in the
distance of our forearms.

I seem to be rude but it's a trick of the passing of
things. We watch a large string of drool fall from between
our steps like we've been holding it inside our chest and
limbs, crumbled apart like a lung: a disemboweled creature
kept as a Thought.
Something has drawn us away from nothing: it is pulsing,
tightening around us now as we increase our speed to catch
up with it.
The objective is to enter each reality, locate its
corresponding limb and limblets and the noise of water now,
humming, approaching and growing louder, like we're back
in our chest. Somewhere on those racks is a sort of psychic
security measure, preventing anything from the forest. But
it's much more work to eat.
There is a sort of psychic phantom limb syndrome, only for
a time. We remember, running, moving ever outward into the
void that supports our body. We remember darkness and the
void is no night, but day is out then and didn't return
until well after it was left in peace.
I hope that you enter into these realities at great cost,
but the imbecilic operator kept placing me on hold, asking
to repeat myself.
If the void was removed, I might become my own Feeling, I
imagined, another something.
When they cut our antlers away. When it becomes everything
again, we flow from gravel into the hardened crust of the
other pieces before ours
Remember the white screen?
The color is so blinding it obliterates the question. The
wheels speeding up, the plant growing, the photo in the
void that supports our body in a cart nearby, removing our
clothing afterwards. We struggle to huff and watch our
fingers through it to find more and more, each time it
cracks, causing us to feel its absence.
Tally long enough to breathe again.

A snout to run toward the interior of the fabric of
reality.
The men in white throws the needle.
In the water it's cold.
We scrape the roughneck bark until an edge is honed.

We are all of these remembrances in the valley of the
valley, like in the distance of our lower limbs to touch my
Pain. We were children, would dip our toes in it.
There's vision in the bird-filled sky to blue and grey we
begin to run. We are moving through it now, there was ever
a place without doors or windows, with nothing at all. The
being begins chanting in a voice so near its hot breath
bleeds upon our limblets.
There is the process—all of it is another face entirely—
covered like black fire. We were in existence without being
in existence as well, seeing it as such.
Time swoops down to our signals and we haven't even time
to study it. Born in the knowledge that soon it will mean
a part of me that's missing. Pain has begun again to feed
an entire crew for an answer rather than nothing, like
something we felt from before the hatching.
Our limbs are culprits: our limbs are culprits: our limbs
and limblets.
In that essence that we've entered the death place. [I
asked him where he finds perfection].
It appears exactly the science behind it. Taste is an enemy
of times before the void, which once was a Time, one unlike
this voidlike Time, another void where Time pushes in its
familiarity.
[The ground I think only now I can't articulate it].
WILL YOU SEE US THEY MAYBE ARE TAKING US TO YOU NOW YOU ARE
IS WHERE I COULD BE BUT WE'RE BOTH JUST OUTSIDE
I catch bits and pieces of who we are, even brood shoal can
swift be supped like we remember. But for me here space
inside us exists only that can be visually verified—Wet
nor Thought nor nothing—it enters our midparts, removing
the barrier we placed there to hinder Pain from falling
down upon the forest and the valley or somewhere else WHY
CAN I FEEL SOMETHING IT ISN'T EVEN YOU'RE JUST OUTSIDE
BRING SOMETHING WITH YOU, OUCH!

We feel and hear; then the world grew.

I think is not light, but darkness; not vision, but the
lack of new clothes, a single solid jacket with which we
once were, where we remained in our madness, summoned
towards this spectral voice.

Things are becoming something. We can remember we have a
clear view of our life with the void once passed and our
ideas fall down upon the air. One only need guess at our
collected stories, the ones found in the storeroom where we
can comfortably grow dim.

Your emptiness is devoid of anything but itself because
there' s nothing now for quite some time.

We haven' t always been spotless children running from a
smell in the developer solution, or some sort of mantra of
their facial structure warped, changed as the voidlings,
welcoming us into a corner of the frozen ice of another
world where men are scarce and terrified.

We were in the valley but in the sense that...that maybe, I
don' t know.

I am nothing, but I can feel that trees hinder my
progression. When can we fully wake and see with our
digits?

For your sake, I hope that you enter into these realities
at great cost, a disemboweled creature kept as a child,
grow to scale our little burn until the limblets on our
right, passing painfully between bearded rocks, slick and
jagged, tearing into us in a vacuum.

Things slowly came into focus...or became lighter, as
if...well, as if to taste the splatlets and the Void Once
Present and the valley.

I don' t know but maybe so.

It was the Poet.

Our greyish fingertips an evidence of the whole, between
my limb in its relation to the other, sometimes creating a
history out of the cosmos, and although I know now, that

the void that supports my mind with my limb; the noise like
spray, something pulling towards us, the herd been running
since forever, we are here where we are. Even brood shoal
can swift be supped like we remember something distant.

At times it howls like a cold, familiar cloak.
In a darkened, dimmer corner of the excrement and
expectorations of all wisdom, they disperse into darkness.
They said it would make the perfect fit on another item that
attracts our attention.
We watch as the forest aided us as well, expanding; our ideas,
limbs, even the voided midparts and items are there; here,
where we plunge deeper into nothing, noising themselves ahead
into nothing; noising themselves ahead into nothing; rightly,
for who are we here, now?
[They must have gotten themselves a trophy this morning].
Now he too, is screaming, much like the fire of the cart.
Our thoughts slow to a strange way to the way they cannot
compete with the tips of our time with senseless questions.
I began to fall.
We lay pressed upon a dark bird, nudging us off our path.
We compare each of its breaths into my snout—my muzzleside
whole body, punched-through flesh—until we can explain.
We awoke from a fitful slumber to a history, the one behind
you closes.
After putting their tools away, they stand at the monumental
amount of delusional disorders that can be something beautiful
since we remember, running, moving ever outward into the void
that once was perhaps.
Somewhere on those racks is a day once passed when in the void
once passed we encountered something like that and spent the
last several days—perhaps more, we' re uncertain—watching
the hair bristle out of focus.
Blown apart eventually, when the candlelight' s extinguished.
We try to bring into ourselves a light devoid of sight and
movement, because sight no longer cares. But we have learned
how to escape from this raunchy palace of the limb shelves.
Surrounding us are others like us are in existence without
being in existence without being in existence without being
in existence without being in existence without being in
existence because of these things with us.

The beginning began as the Pain we felt once passed, again
into the void moments passed.
We have plotted our expansion out into the proper place
because we're afraid to say. For what is an idea above our
heads as we enter the forest floor?
Upon the walls of shadowed night into the doctor's
shattered space, the man in white grows ever blinding
like our limbs. We are crafting a map that can present
themselves beneath my void in front of me.
I'd like to think outside of the surrounding room.
I'm different from the candle blown out.
We were in the valley of the Feeling.
You've rearranged the furniture—so to speak—and now the
soundfeeling subsides, green, and we falter for a moment
and the herd must bound back then around away from the
void that supports our body; these voidlings scattered
throughout the void had something to be: a white bed,
housing what we could never reach.
The doctor told us today we're never getting out of it,
it's permeated with the heard. He is a builder of things,
trying to rob me of something.
Did we hear this noise brings this Thought too has
something to keep us from the voidling; its screams travel
through these various realities, were also designed with a
clatter.
It's something I recognize.
But it seems to take a deep sort of psychic security
measure, preventing anything from the candle out.
But it must be many hunters, mixed together with the
ancient one's moldy bones, a monument unanswered.
Time passes days night years counts only by light one by
one, salting the pieces of us it must be there, for we know
that not everything was nothing, or we ourselves now fail
to mark.
[Eaten back into inexplicable darkness].

We feel our restraints burst. Not quite Pain nor Nothing,
but it is I who will help them escape. Our sallow yellowed
arm, the rest of them who've ever lived.
The empty spots about us, devoid of sight and movement,
because sight no longer marks, living off our warmth
somewhere inside.
This time the Pain is blinding, but the rewards are
unimaginable.
We feel ourselves dropped back upon the forest to open up
in our relation to the cave.

It is leading us to own this darkness.
It was almost imperceptible, but the rewards are
unimaginable.
This time the right one.
Blow the candle and stood up and down us as they continue
down onto the void once passed.
There was something...it was something that seems like ages
and none of us a river is running.
Between our bewildered screams we pass the Time—this is
something to be torn into pieces.
These ones bear some vague resemblance to people we
feel again the voidlings beneath our limbs seems to be
extracted, unlocked, and lived perhaps, once again, another
splat.
But close to our eyes and it feels like Pain is everywhere,
as if some sort of different, indescribable quality: a
Sensation, I think, gathering up the other supports our
body, nearby.
The Great Philosopher King, who ushered his children out
of the doctor shifts our head is we think we feel it where
it all seems so short now and realizing that to exist for
us; it's a sort of psychic security measure, preventing
anything from the void that once a time there are items to
keep from spilling out again and approaches us.
Even still: the sound it made.
Still we stay, to listen for something; to see if there are
noises outside the room itself.
Returning also poses the risk of being stranded in that
stage I described earlier...as waiting for rain, though
there's hardly little stake in it save for the sake of
something.
From the wetness of the animals that were unnoticeable
at our collected stories, the ones that come apart, are
soft and pale with piercing ice blue eyes, then the ground
its spray Memory like we are elsewhere going here and

everywhere, floating thrashing flitting into light.
Eaten back into familiar darkness.
The doctor told us today we're never getting out of the
swarm, in the forest?
He does the meaning of loss.
For if there are other parts of your journey, or at a
future date as you see it?
We are unable to return.
But the beauty was, I could see he was more naive, so we
continue forwards.
And now I can quite...
The chant is now blocked.
But there was a remarkable success rate with a hard thud.
At first, there was ever a place in my head, like it was
everything.

We have this: there are only bits and pieces of who we are,
split between many bodies and worlds, sewn together for
some reason.
It was the perfect fit on another item I'm shouting out
loud but there's no pause—no hesitation—for the piss of
death and the sound that stalks us now.
I can't feel it where it used to say: little lives unto
themselves.
That shadow from the voidling excretes a noise nearby.
I find it in an uproar as the man we recognize—at least by
his looks—but it is cold, but why?
If so, our existence gives it power.
The cold is almost overpowering—one part of the infirm and
they cut away layer and layer of the matter beneath us;
beneath our dirty sheets.
Night is made for small fry, and we see upon it with limb
and limblet.
I can tell from life painting sodden ground below, our life
once lived, it warms us.
If you are dead?
It was all too easy to tear it out into air we breath,
it's moist and cold.
The flavors of a pudding cup, as if for a moment, the tilts
our head but the Thought of it.
The void was as it relies upon the wind cracks and the herd
kept track of the limb shelves.
But I think is not the THE BED BALL BELOW THE BED & ONLY US
& THE BALL why aren't you here? you were following us when
it starts, it's empty.
One of the cart.
But even now, the birds.
Somewhere on those racks is a trick I read of once in a
memory, the iron smell of death.
We can no longer bound about as freely; the sour smell
still burning.

It excreted a little life once lived?
He shrugged and went out then and our ideas such that one
floats above our head.
But we can hear me...
Soup stretched into every meal, thinning entirely until
becoming nothing more than a void, or more so than before.
It was my own personal void.
A vegetal stench we squeeze between our frosty digits, like
nothing.

It's a Ground because we Feel with our cloven memories
behind, we inch our way out of doors was always drawn
toward the bird-filled sky?
Could you see yourselves to let them spill in, out, in, out
of fear and terror.
We try to find something beyond it.
When all is it?
None of this sound?
Never did we come across something.
We begin our procession deeper into nothing.
Do you hear it in the room where we're installed.
Alright, if you think so?
The architect pauses for a living, to be marked; touched
and invaded.
The Stories from the bird-filled sky?
PSYCHIC MAP ATTACHMENT To facilitate travel through these
various realities, were also designed with a thud and they
remain.
Only I can only reply in answer to such thoughts, a noise
we can prove such existence.
The glimpses appear infrequently and when it presses
against our midparts.
And when it has been soldered over with pink flesh.
A blindness and refusal of the brain, then the bed and
thing around his neck when they entered and I mark them
thusly.
And now, screeching our stories in the air, a voice upon
the wind says: *See?*

The child comes with the growing of the light, several
meters ahead of us he stops and beckons, begins inching
forward, our body still frozen into ice, and so it turns,
waits who knows how long, until the ice begins to melt, the
smell of water and death, beside us, a river, waters
rushing, pushing up the banks as the land surrounding thaws
into the faint light, a period of time drawn out and
unchanging, but the light is there, remains high, shrouded
in mist, and once the ice begins melting the child takes a
step away, one step away from us at a time, and, as the ice
melts, more; another, then another, and our vision begins
to fade until all that remains is the memory of a candle in
the sky but with the child, the rising of the light,
there' s an urgency, the glow, an itching in our bones and
at first, the cold is nearly overpowering, the rays of
light frigid, distant, but the ice begins to melt, a part
of us telling us we' re frozen but our exterior seems
unaffected, another part feeling the pain, stiff and frozen
limbs waking beneath the ice, which too is waking,
groaning, cracking all around us, waking with the child and
the light, awakening with the vision of awaking, not
returning, struggling to lift ourselves, and in the
distance, the child watches, stepping cautiously an inch
away at a time, from what it sees or from nothing really,
or anything—from us—we' re not sure, from the slow
shifting deep below, the Earth waking itself after a long
and sleepless dream, the churning void—that' s the word—
the churning air, impenetrably thick, the stench of rot a
vision now, whether it' s us we' re unsure, but there, the
child stands watching us, the air cold and fresh in our
lungs, the horrific smell that calls for verification, and
we struggle against the ice, encased in it, exhausting
ourselves to see, blinding like a glow going through our
bodies off to somewhere else, and time knows thought so
well, knows that it takes a history to truly open one' s

eyes, a history for the blindness slowly dissolving, but
the child waits for what? the wind rips a great, steady
drone, crystals of snow and ice carving our face into a
lunar landscape, this is the ringing in the ears, we think,
then take a deep breath, until everything melts we are a
part of it and inside of us is a sort of strange sensation,
the parts which form our existence—the physical one—still
continuing to develop, this ice, our encasement, another
crumb of whatever one would call a being and as the ice
melts, the child moves further away, one step at a time,
and it knows us, it knows us well, and there' s more now
inside of us than we' ve been given license to, things
we' ve collected following us everywhere, encapsulated
until the Earth grew sane again, or no? the strange
sensation, the development of other parts, parts once
black, insubstantial, underexposed or overexposed, blowing
out into nothing, returning as ideas like a thin white film
wrapping around a spool, which is the part of us that
remains, and the child takes another step and the horizon
shudders, ideas called up, tighten like a corset around our
chest, joining history, fusing to where we were—where we
are now—solidifying, the stench of decay becoming a
familiar, a sort of strange sensation dancing up and down
our limbs buried deep within the ice, a story continuing
even now, shaping a nature, an exit with everything we' ve
collected, a stone gathering dust to become a mountain
upside down in the forest, and the child, blonde and
unattainable, the ideal, an insect burrowing beneath the
skin in a passing moment, a bite that awakens us, a day
with light, floating belly upwards, completely out of
control—simply floating—dissolving into what surrounds
us, and the child takes another step and the vision fades,
then returns forcefully, skin flaking away, dried out,
hanging horribly like a wet towel, the weight of it making
our eyes water, aging a hole inside our head replaced with

distrust, riddled with demons, bones reading the coming of
the rain, flexed with the age of meaning, the child's hair
glows like the sun, like a candle, as the ice breaks away
we stumble toward the glow, is it the sun? the cave we'd
swept away? heat exuding from our limbs and the horizon
judders and disappears, and the child takes another step,
we stumble toward a dream and the light grows stronger, our
frame gains momentum, the blur of bodies line the banks,
the water tame, soft yet flowing, bearing no reflection of
ourselves; we stop to consider this, then turn, and there,
the blonde child, a face we also know, begins running, our
vision swept away like rushing water, disappearing in
returning, a momentary blindness, so we stumble forward
more quickly, stretching ever for the candle's glow, and
in an instant, our vision returns; eventually, the
stumbling becomes a run, the feeling of the way it once
was, the landscape a blur, meeting the air moving forward
in a slice, the wind hot and cold upon our ears, pricking,
the child a good pace ahead of us as the sweat drips down,
soaking our fur, our being, crusting it back into ice along
with the smell of death—the bodies—inescapable but
familiar, we turn to find a being running beside us,
gesticulating wildly, without language, it continues,
dirty, malformed, maneuvering as a bird flaps its wings,
rippling its whole body, the image dissolving and coming
back together again, something like a lake not a mirror,
the reflection pulled apart before taking the plunge and
placing the apple in its mouth, and we stand there caught,
gazing too at what ripples like heat upon the horizon, and
our vision fades and now the child is far ahead of us,
leaving us behind in our vanity, and we surrender and
continue, stumbling forward like a yew fresh from the womb,
running but tripping over a root caught underfoot, and down
we go, down into darkness, vision snuffed out like a votive
candle, the blackness we know so well, the impenetrable

comfort of nothingness, remaining only briefly, and after a
time we feel the light, the glow of the candle driving us
forward, a warm ladle scooping us up, so we rise from the
darkness, still blind and stumbling, running forward,
brushing against the crumbling bodies along the banks—ones
we'd touched before unknowingly—chasing the memory of the
candle until after a time, the light reveals itself to us
and we're staring at the child on the horizon, hair like
golden flax catching in the wind, the sound of rushing
water fills our ears and we turn again, glancing back at
the river, growing in intensity as the ice continues
melting and we continue running, trying to catch up to the
child to see if it's really what we think it is, or what
we thought it could be; trying to see if it's really like
anything we think it could be—these ideas—bubbling
upwards out of the void in the shape of the sun or an egg
tied to the string of a child's blue balloon, if they'd
only slow down we'd ruffle their flaxen hair perhaps and
give it to them to see if they're really what we think
they are, if they're really doing what we think they're
doing, but the corpses that line the banks get in the way
too often, though we keep the glow in front of us, the
pressure's changing, we feel it in our limbs, the sun
trying to rise, chasing the child like a wolf, wild with a
sense of unknowing as the dead ice cracks beneath our feet
in a fractured timeline, a living reflection of a body in a
mirror with worms for brains, as we run we pass a quiet
spot in the water, along the bank, a body, its arms in the
water, brushing the waving moss of a rock, face frozen in a
horrible grimace, we rush by it and it falls apart,
collapses, the head rocking forwards, floating away, a face
like cracked leather, did we know them? are they one of us
now? the color green, we think, then our vision shudders
again and the blonde child's there before us, closer now
than ever, and we know the past exists inside of us, not

behind us, the thought of pages being torn from a book and
thrown upon a fire arises out of nowhere, then is gone, and
ahead the candlelight grows ever stronger, we're gaining
distance, so we continue, running forwards, bentback knees,
lilting at understanding, imagining a pathway surrounded by
tall grass, cut along into the bank of another river, never
knowing whether the water would forgive us or not, and we
see now clearly that the child wears a green cape, almost
melting into the air as it runs, reminding us of the smell
of life, and in front of us, the child trips, we reach out
and grasp its cape but it slips, revealing a severed arm
before they're back on their feet, running again, making
our vision fade slightly, the wind still whipping by our
ears, the ice melting and howling beneath our limbs, the
steam rushing into the air hazing out the light until the
horizon begins growing dark, and a thought trails behind
us, inflated like a balloon caught unsteadily in the wind,
and now, it occurs to us to speak, so we shout "stop!"
and the child skids in the ice-covered muck, making a sound
like dragging a wet stick through sand, and turns to look
at us, and for the first time we see its face, beautiful
and golden with eyes as black as night, and we stop running
and stand beside the bank, the rushing of the water
building into a torrent, and the child approaches and we
wait, watching its green cape fluttering in the wind, and
when it reaches us, it's as if we've finally flown into
the candle, like we've always wanted; we reach out our
hands, stroke the child's hair as they stand there,
unafraid; we place our limbs around its neck, gripping it
around the throat, and the child doesn't resist, and in
another moment its body begins to shake, so we stare into
those black eyes and finally we see, unsteady and inhumanly
beautiful, our visage for the first time, pieced together
by the rotten age of centuries, we admire ourselves as the
throbbing, black orbs bulge, pulsing with an outward force

and the child's body goes limp, staring until all that
remains in front of us are two large, black orbs, melting
together into one, into a deep, impenetrable pool, viscous
with our reflection, shimmering, then growing dimmer,
fading away as if steam in the air, a remnant of light
pressed upon the eyelids, fading away, deepening, plunging
into the darkness, returning; we try to say something but
before it can escape our mouth, a bubble pops, and then
there's nothing.

...but the void

Daniel Beauregard lives in Buenos Aires, Argentina. His work has appeared or is forthcoming in a number of places including *Propagule, ergot, Selffuck, New South, Burning House Press, Alwayscrashing*, and elsewhere. He's the author of numerous chapbooks of poetry, most recently *Total Darkness Means No Notifications* (Anstruther Press) and *Anatomizing Uncanny Alley* (Selffuck). His full-length collection of poetry, *You Alive Home Yet?* is available from Schism Neuronics and his splatterpunk novel *Blood Pudding* from World Castle Publishing. His post-apocalyptic novella *The Mother of Flowers* is available from The Wild Rose Press, and his first collection of short stories, *Funeralopolis* (Orbis Tertius Press) will be published in 2023. Daniel is also co-founder of OOMPH!, a small press devoted to the publication of poetry and prose in translation. He can be reached on Twitter @666ICECREAM.

PUBLISHED BY ERRATUM REPRINTS

The Scourge of Villanie
John Marston

Civilisation Its Cause and Cure
Edward Carpenter

www.ingramcontent.com/pod-product-compliance
Lightning Source LLC
Chambersburg PA
CBHW051135190726
48290CB00006B/1851